Walking into the Night

Walking
into the Night

Olaf Olafsson

Pantheon Books, New York

Many thanks to Victoria Cribb
for her invaluable assistance when writing this book.

Copyright © 2003 by Double O Investment Corporation

All rights reserved under International and Pan-American Copyright
Conventions. Published in the United States by Pantheon Books,
a division of Random House, Inc., New York.

Pantheon Books and colophon are registered trademarks
of Random House, Inc.

Library of Congress Cataloging-in-Publication Data

Ólafur Jóhann Ólafsson.
Walking into the night / Olaf Olafsson.
p.   cm.
ISBN 0-375-42254-4
1. Icelandic Americans—Fiction.   2. Hearst, William Randolph,
1863–1951—Fiction.   3. San Simeon (Calif.)—Fiction.   4. Loss
(Psychology)—Fiction.   5. Runaway husbands—Fiction.
6. Butlers—Fiction.   I. Title.

PS3615.L34W35 2003   839'.6934—dc21   2003048812
www.pantheonbooks.com

Book design by Johanna S. Roebas

Printed in the United States of America

First Edition

2   4   6   8   9   7   5   3   1

Acknowledgments

While some of the characters who appear in this novel are based on historical figures, it is important to stress that my portrayal of them is strictly fictional. I am, however, indebted to the brothers Arni Tomas and Kristjan Tomas Ragnarsson, who so generously shared with me their grandfather's story as well as letters, journals, and reminiscences, without which this book could not have been written.

I must also take this opportunity to thank my editor, Carol Brown Janeway, for her thorough reading of the book and her advice; my agent, Gloria Loomis, for her care and support; and, last but not least, my dear friend Jason Epstein, whose guidance and wisdom I have had the privilege of enjoying for many years.

The cypress rested in its shadow.

He tripped on the steps up to the main building but managed not to fall. Fuchsia blossoms met his eye as he straightened up; azaleas beyond them. He walked over to the cypress and leaned against it while he caught his breath. He was hot in his black suit in the afternoon sun. Reaching into his pocket, he took out a white handkerchief to mop his brow and pat his cheeks. Fair-weather clouds hovered on the horizon, while closer to shore gleaming ripples tossed back and forth. He sensed a breeze, and suddenly a sharp whistling sound passed through the trees and a bell clanged in one of the towers. Once, then silence. He noticed a hint of lavender as he put the handkerchief back in his pocket and continued on his way.

The Chief had mislaid his magnifying glass. Kristjan—or, rather, Christian Benediktsson, as he had called himself since coming to this country during the Great War, twenty years ago—had spent the morning hunting for it in the old man's bedroom and on the balcony outside, in the gothic library next door and down in the reception room, first by the teletype machine, then on the jigsaw-puzzle and chess tables, but without success. He had paused in his search for a moment when the teletype suddenly began to hum, and hesitated before the machine, waiting for the message the Chief had been expecting.

"What on earth can have happened to that magnifying glass, Christian?" asked the old man as his butler handed him the telegram and reported his failure. The Chief glanced at the message, then went to the window and said: "Unless I left it outside yesterday."

Kristjan thought he remembered seeing his employer wandering around the previous afternoon with a book in his hand, Dickens, he believed, as it had the same leather binding as the collected works. *Oliver Twist* had been lying on the Chief's bedside table yesterday morning but was there no longer, so it seemed likely to have been the one. He had looked round all the guesthouses, by the Neptune Pool, in the billiards room, where he remembered seeing the Chief sitting for a while before sunset yesterday, by the fountain with the statue of David, and in Miss Davies' room, though she hadn't been there for over a week and wasn't expected until next weekend, when the Chief was planning a costume ball.

Had he thoroughly checked by the swimming pool? He stopped in his tracks, trying to remember whether he'd looked under the table on the side where the old man usually sat. He didn't move on again until he'd convinced himself that he had missed nothing.

The magnifying glass was of medium size, with an ivory handle gilt-embossed with the Chief's initials: WRH. He had borne it a grudge ever since the Chief fell asleep in his poolside chair last year with a book on his lap, the magnifying glass clutched in his right hand over an open page. Kristjan had been in the house fetching a cold drink for Miss Davies when he heard the screams.

He set off immediately at a trot, trying to balance the drink on its silver tray, through sunbeams and shadows, and dropped the glass at the sight of the Chief lurching to his feet with his jacket in flames. The book lay burning on the edge of the pool at his feet but he was still clutching the magnifying glass. He seemed dazed with sleep, so Kristjan grabbed him round the waist and leaped into the pool with him.

It was remarkable that the Chief had only slightly singed the back of his right hand but otherwise escaped unharmed. Once he'd grasped what had happened, he stroked his shirt where it had caught fire, and said:

"Where were you?"

Kristjan put an arm under his shoulder and helped him up onto the side of the pool, where Miss Davies was waiting for them. The gardener and two girls from the kitchen, who had rushed out when they heard the screams, now retreated out of sight so the Chief wouldn't realize they had witnessed his humiliation.

"Where were you?" he repeated.

"He was just fetching me some lemonade, dear."

She helped him indoors while Kristjan swept up the charred remains of the book and picked up pieces of glass from the path where he had dropped the drink. He worked methodically, taking care not to cut his fingers or burn himself on the still smoldering book. *Oliver Twist,* a first edition, bound in light-brown leather. Before going inside to change, he emptied the water from his shoes.

Kristjan quickened his pace. The hunt for the magnifying glass had disrupted his day. He pulled the watch from his pocket and squinted at it. Half past two. Monday—May 17th. "San Simeon, May 22nd, 1937," was engraved at the top of the menu for Saturday night's dinner. He'd found two spelling errors and had them corrected. The Chief's shoes were waiting to be polished and he still had to make a clean copy of the guest list for the costume ball. A cool draft sneaked from the shadows, and for a moment he imagined someone was breathing on his neck. He started.

"Klara," he whispered. "Is that you again?"

It was by accident that he found it on his way back to the house. A glimmer caught his eye on his way past the four statues of Sekhmet, the lion-faced Egyptian goddess of war and battle; a flicker on the balcony behind her. What a relief! He couldn't wait to bring it to the Chief.

He wiped the dust off the handle and polished the glass with his handkerchief as he hurried back to the main building. It was getting cooler but he didn't notice. In the distance the sky was darkening. A whistling breeze swept over the hill but the cypress caught it. The bell clanged. He knew the Chief would be pleased to see his magnifying glass again.

He lay on his back covered by a thin sheet. It was still hot; he slept naked. The window was open but in the corner a dim light burned; he had switched it on before getting into bed. For years he had been unable to sleep in the dark.

The lion in the Chief's zoo had been restless tonight. He imagined it pacing in its cage. In his dream he saw fog over the bay and mist on the hillsides; in the moonlight it looked like newly fallen snow.

He slept lightly, his hands resting at his sides. The glow cast by the lamp crawled up the sheet, fading out over his chest and leaving his face in darkness, apart from a splash of light on his forehead. He was nearing fifty but people still commented on his striking looks. Fair, broad shouldered, of medium height, his hands powerful despite the long, fine fingers. He still had to restrain his thick, wiry hair.

His room was two doors down the hallway from Mr. Hearst's bedroom. He had not spent a single night in the servant's quarters since he first came here, for the Chief wanted him close by. He usually slept with his door ajar so he could hear if the old man called for him. Tonight, however, he had shut it as Mr. Hearst was away and not due back until tomorrow. But Miss Davies had appeared just before supper, taking everyone by surprise. They had thought she would be in Los Angeles until Friday. She was alone.

Tomorrow morning a ship was due to dock at the San Simeon quay, carrying iron, cement, and steel. The Chief had asked him to supervise the unloading, as he suspected he had been cheated on the last consignment. Kristjan was looking forward to spending the day down by the sea.

The smell of the ocean came through the window and he turned his head towards it as if he sensed it in his sleep. The fingers of his left hand twitched a little, then his body grew calm again and his breathing slowed and became regular, though now and then his eyelids flickered. Lately his dreams had taken him to the small village in Iceland where he'd grown up. To the jetty and the mountain behind the village. He had no idea why and didn't think his dreams were of any significance.

He didn't wake up when she opened the door and entered. Leaving it ajar behind her, she stopped by his bed and looked at him. The curtains fluttered; the shape of his body was visible under the sheet.

Gradually Kristjan became aware of her presence, though she remained where she was without moving, simply watching him. Slowly he opened his eyes, blinking as he grew accustomed to the light, then turned his head in her direction.

"Is that you?" he asked.

She was wearing a white silk robe, her arms folded. She wore her strawberry blond hair long, in flowing curls. Her eyes were bright blue, her smile girlish when she wanted it to be. She held a cigarette in a holder between her index and middle fingers, as if she had forgotten it was there. Her fingers were short and pink, the holder long and white with a gold ring around the end that held the cigarette.

"What did you say?" she asked quietly. "Was that Icelandic?"

It took him a while to shrug off his sleep, as though something was dragging at him from the depths of a dream.

"Oh, it's you, Miss Davies," he said at last. "Is something wrong?"

"There's nothing wrong."

If she reached out her hand she could brush against his skin. They were both aware of this.

"Who did you think it was?"

"I was dreaming . . ."

"About who?"

He didn't answer.

"A woman?"

He rose up on his elbow.

"I was dreaming. Is there something wrong?"

She smiled. Her own smile, not a smile from one of her movies.

"I wanted the guest list for Saturday. If you wouldn't mind . . ."

He stretched under the sheet, looking at her abstractedly, a white figure in the quiet half-darkness.

"It's down in the kitchen. I'll go get it."

She didn't move.

"I'll bring it to you . . ."

He smelled her breath as she finally turned her back on him and went to the door. He wasn't surprised that she had managed to get her hands on a bottle; the Chief wasn't home to keep an eye on her. The smell was faint and not unpleasant.

She turned at the door.

"Christian," she said. "I can't sleep. The lion's been roaring all night. Can you do something about it?"

She was ten years younger than Kristjan, twenty-five years younger than Hearst, who had met her when she was an eighteen-year-old chorus girl on Broadway. He was still married to his wife, who was living on the East Coast. They had five sons. Miss Davies was now a movie star.

"I'll get the list," he said. "Then I think you should try to get some sleep."

He stepped slowly out of bed when she had gone and stood by the window for a long time before pulling on his clothes.

The lion was silent again.

San Simeon, May 20, 1937

My darling Elisabet!

I haven't forgotten my promise to try to explain what happened. It's going to be difficult, that's for certain, because I often doubt if I understand it myself. By saying this I'm not trying to excuse myself, you mustn't think that. I know that you deserve better.

He wrote slowly, putting down the pen from time to time, screwing on the cap, his eyes distracted, as if he were trying to remember the nuances of a voice that had long since fallen silent. He sat like this for a long while, until at last he grew restless in his seat and strained his ears. He had opened the door to the balcony; a warm breeze lifted the paper on the table before him, then set it down again, carefully as if not to disturb him. The windows and balcony door were open, creating a cross-draft for the Chief, who was having trouble again with his breathing that night.

"My *darling* Elisabet," he wrote without hesitation. He had changed the salutation in the first two letters as well, so they would all begin in the same way. For a long time he had been unsure whether to use that delicate word—*darling,* whether it would seem impertinent or arrogant. Perhaps this was why he had given up when he first tried to write to her nearly four years ago. It had disturbed him that he had not even been able to find a way to address her. But now he was comfortable with the word and could place it before her name effortlessly, even with enjoyment, finding it a source of solace, murmuring the words softly like a prayer.

He had written the first letter about a month ago. This was the third.

This morning, when I was taking the Chief his breakfast out on what's known as the Tea Terrace, I suddenly started thinking about our first year at Eyrarbakki. When was it—1908? 1909? It was 1909, wasn't it? Completely out of the blue I remembered our morning walks along the beach before I went to the office and you sat down at the piano. I was wondering whether we really took those walks every day, but can't quite remember, though I'm pretty sure it must have been at least every other day. I'm sure we used to walk along the beach whatever the time of year; yet I can only picture us in brilliant sunshine . . .

He suddenly lost the thread, feeling for a moment suspended in midair. He had been about to recall how small he had found Eyrarbakki after his return from Copenhagen, how he had wanted them to move directly to Reykjavik. These Icelandic villages, he had thought to himself, everyone with their nose in everybody else's business, like a little prison in the midst of the great empty landscape. But he stopped himself. These letters to Elisabet were hardly the right place for such reflections. No, I must keep a hold on myself, he thought, I mustn't let myself get agitated.

He stood up to calm his mind. He heard footsteps on the terrace, went out onto the balcony and watched one of the kitchen girls walking down the hill. "It was the footsteps," he told himself, "that's what distracted me." They faded but he could still hear the crunching of sand on a beach.

I seem to remember that we still took our morning walks when you were pregnant with Einar, at least during the first few months, but I can't remember whether we stopped altogether after that or started again later on. Somehow I think we gave up the habit before Maria was born, as it was not long afterwards that we moved to Reykjavik. In 1912. God, it's all such a long time ago.

"Such a long time ago," he repeated to himself in the quiet of the evening and chose to leave it at that rather than acknowledge how many years it had been. He gripped the balcony rail with both hands, leaned forward, then straightened up and went inside.

The pale moon had risen above the ragged mountains. He remembered that he had once told her he could trace her footprints in the newly fallen moonlight, but decided this was not the time to remind her of that.

Just as he was about to sit down again he heard his name echoing in the hallway. Twice, louder the second time.

"Christian!"

The Chief could easily have pressed the button beside his bed that rang the bell in his butler's room, but he never did. "Christian!" he would call, drawing out the last syllable, until his manservant arrived.

During the early years he had put on his jacket before attending to the Chief, adjusting his tie and glancing in the mirror to make sure he was presentable, but now he went out in his shirt-sleeves, stopping only to button his cuffs, which he had loosened earlier, and brushing some pollen off one trouser leg, though more from habit than any sense of duty.

Though the Chief heard his approaching footsteps, he called out once more, as if to confirm his need and his power.

On a table in an alcove stood two bronze lions, along with various other bits and pieces—a cigarette case, a vase, and an antique spoon with a broken handle. One of the lions held up a card with the name of the month, the other the date: May 20. He paused beside them, suddenly realizing what had been nagging at his memory for the last couple of days. May 20th. Maria would be twenty-five tomorrow.

He shook his head inadvertently, as if to fend off an unexpected attack. His ears rang but he carried on regardless, pushing open the door to the Chief's bedroom and entering the gloomy half-darkness with slow steps.

High up in the oak by the walkway outside my window bluebirds have made their nest. I watch their comings and goings through a pair of binoculars whenever I have time; there are four chicks in the nest. Yesterday the male made eighteen journeys in just half an hour for food. He never seemed to come home empty-handed, if you can say that of a bird. I've been trying to draw them but have lost some of my old skill through lack of practice. I always thought the drawing I did of the black-tailed godwit—the one we hung in the study—was best. I remember how hard it was to capture the shadings of its chestnut breast; it's as though I was working on it only yesterday. It was around noon on a Saturday. The sound of hammering drifted in through the window, the smell of pancakes carried from the kitchen, and I looked up to see Maria closing the gate to the street and strolling up the path to the house. She looked dreamy, and paused on the way; I seem to remember she was holding a buttercup in her hand . . .

But now I'm out of practice and can't capture the blue sheen on the birds' backs and wings, even though I can picture it and know it from the sea and the sky. In fact, I came across a dead bird down on the hillside the other day and brought it home so I wouldn't have to rely on my faulty memory. But it didn't work—there was no way I could find the right shade, even with my new watercolors.

The steamer I wrote you about will leave tomorrow morning. The warehouses are now packed with iron and cement for the Chief's endless building projects here on the hill. I dreamed last night that I sailed away with the ship; I was wearing the blue hat I bought in Copenhagen, waving from the deck. I've dreamed this dream before but this time I woke up disoriented because it's years since I've seen that hat or even thought about it. Could I have left it behind?

He folded the letter carefully; five densely written sheets, a polished, almost feminine hand, in blue ink. He didn't date it and wrote nothing on the envelope but her name. He didn't seal it but opened the bottom drawer of the desk and laid it on top of the other two letters, next to a small boat whittled from a piece of wood that bore the name *Einar RE 1* and a pebble from home. He laid it carefully on top of the other two letters and decided not to wonder if he would ever send them.

Beneath the peaks of the Santa Lucia range, a few miles inland from the coast, rises the castle built by William Randolph Hearst. Seventeen years ago, before Hearst arrived with his plans, there was nothing on these hills but sunbaked gravel, the odd oak that had managed to put down roots, laurel and sage, and, on the lower slopes, winding, rutted cattle tracks and dry creek beds which ran out in the middle of the plain, having abandoned the attempt to reach the sea. During winter and spring the low-lying land is green, but the grass bleaches during the summer and turns yellow by fall. The shore is lined with sandy beaches, rocks, dunes, and bluffs. The village of San Simeon, with its fish-drying frames, boats, and fishermen's shacks, so empty and silent it seems even the Almighty has overlooked it, lies a stone's throw to the north.

The summer heat can become unbearable down on the plain, but up in the hills the air is cooler. In the spring the wind sweeps like a white wing over the sand and flats, but in the winter it howls and rages. Sometimes when he can't sleep he remembers the nights when Einar crawled into his bed, afraid that a ghost was blowing on a blade of grass outside his window.

The Chief had printed a leaflet containing information he wanted the staff to tell guests about the place. He calls it the Ranch, and the hill the Enchanted Hill. The staff are never allowed to use the word *castle* to refer to the place. The information sheet notes that first to be built were the three guesthouses, the Casas del Mar, del Sol, and del Monte. In parentheses: "a total of eighteen bedrooms and twenty bathrooms." The print is small, so that everything will fit on one page. Kristjan has advised two waiters with poor eyesight to learn the information by heart so they don't have to squint at it in front of visitors. There are one hundred and fifteen rooms in the main building: fourteen sitting rooms, twenty-six bedrooms, two libraries, thirty fireplaces, a beauty parlor, a barbershop, and a movie theater. The refectory, which is what Hearst calls the dining room, is said to be over three thousand square feet, which Kristjan believes is probably accurate because it takes him about forty seconds to walk the length of the room when he's not in a hurry. The leaflet makes no mention of the service wing, where the staff live, nor the secure vaults in the cellar, though it's mentioned that there is a switchboard and telegraph facility in the construction foreman's office. Kristjan finds the descriptions of the two swimming pools—the indoor bath, which is known as the Roman Pool, and the other, which is named after the sea god Neptune—unnecessarily detailed, but that doesn't seem to bother the guests, whose appetite for information is insatiable. Kristjan welcomes them on the south stairs and escorts them to the rooms they've been assigned while the houseboys bring in their bags. Generally guests arrive ill-equipped for their stay on the hill, especially actors and other movie types from Hollywood. The staff provides them with toiletries, tooth powder and brushes, cologne, combs and razors, perfumes, and all manner of unguents, riding clothes, bathrobes, and bathing suits. It takes about five minutes to fill them in about the place, longer if they're curious. Some ask if they can keep the information sheet but that's against the rules. However, they're always left with the day's menu and a schedule of mealtimes, along with a short description of the movie to be screened that evening.

The Chief's a stickler for rules and order. Many people find him intimidating.

The leaflet once contained a fairly detailed description of the main building but when Mr. Hearst saw it he had it removed. It's called Casa Grande. All vistas lead to where it stands at the top of the hill, with the guesthouses clustered in a semicircle a little lower down, like ladies-in-waiting at the feet of their queen. Some say it resembles a gothic cathedral, its chalk walls corpse white, the campaniles towering grandly aloft, as if their peals were intended more for heaven than for us here below on earth.

Guests have to come to the main building for food and drink as there are no kitchens or refrigerators in the guesthouses. Not even a kettle. The occasional person gets up the nerve to complain about this after a drink or two, though never directly to the Chief. Some would prefer breakfast in bed but the Chief regards this as a waste of time. It's good for people to have a breath of fresh air in the morning, he feels. To walk here in the dew with the sun sparkling on the sea below and a refreshing breeze blowing off the mountains. It's good for them. This is no place for lazybones, he's fond of saying.

Down by the harbor there are warehouses full of antiques and works of art that the Chief has amassed. There are even more warehouses in New York, where people are employed in inventorying and cataloguing the vast quantity of statues, swords, torchères, fireplaces, paintings, tea sets, altarpieces, columns, and vases which Mr. Hearst keeps buying, even though no more can be accommodated here in the houses on the hill. Sometimes he buys whole castles in Spain and Italy and has them demolished stone by stone and strut by strut so they can be loaded on board ship.

So here I am in this labyrinth, Elisabet dear, he wrote, deciding to put the description of the castle into the envelope with the letter, a bird of passage that has lost its way. I'll always be a stranger here, so there is little to remind me of what I miss, and this makes it easier for me to discipline my thoughts. Though I can still be caught unawares. It doesn't take much, no more than the outline of a pale cheek glimpsed through the trees. I try to perform my duties diligently and occupy my mind with as many small details as I can, because it makes the time pass faster and prevents things from stealing into my mind.

It's very peaceful here late in the evening and you never know what visitations may take place in the silence. But I have nothing to complain of, least of all to you.

The Chief is calling. Sometimes I think everyone is afraid of him except me. I'm afraid of nothing but myself.

I see now that I may have given a misleading picture of this establishment and my life here on the hill. I see I called it a "labyrinth," but on reflection I don't think this word gives the right impression. The truth is that I've mostly been happy here, but perhaps I chose not to write that to you, perhaps I felt subconsciously that you would be more likely to forgive me if I told you I'd been miserable all along. Why do I do this? I ask myself. Will I always feel like a naughty child in relation to you? Even now I find it difficult to tell you what I'm thinking for fear that you will disapprove.

I know I wouldn't have stayed this long anywhere else. When I first came here in 1921, I felt as if a whole new world was opening up before me. And at the same time the old one disappeared. It was as if this labyrinth had been built expressly for me to lose myself in, and I managed to do so successfully for years.

Life here used to be one long round of parties. On weekends there were never fewer than twenty people, mostly guests from Hollywood, friends of Miss Davies. You'll have read about these people in the papers and seen them in films: Clark Gable, Rudolph Valentino, Gary Cooper, Chaplin, etc., etc. Sometimes I felt as if I was in a movie with them. These people liked me and turned to me for advice about all sorts of things, especially in relation to the Chief. No one wanted to offend him.

I enjoyed the way the guests deferred to me and I did nothing to play down my relationship with the Chief, though I never bragged about it. I said as little as possible and let people draw their own conclusions. "Do you think it would be all right to go horseback riding this evening?" "Could I borrow a bathing costume?" "Would you be so kind as to get this script to the Chief? I'm sure he'll want to finance the picture if he reads it."

No one knew what I'd done before coming here, no one wondered at my being a servant; on the contrary they looked up to me as people often do here with Europeans. "Iceland?" they would ask. "Where's that again?" They thought it was quite something when the Chief answered for me and said I was a true Viking.

I was always busy. I never gave myself time to let my thoughts wander. I knew that if I did, the memories would flood over me. During the week the building work went on from morning to night; it's still in progress, the Chief's forever extending or altering. On Fridays Miss Davies would generally set off from Los Angeles with her companions; they'd travel through the night, arriving early on Saturday morning. We'd have their breakfast ready; afterwards they'd go to bed and rise again at noon; lunch would be served at half past two. After that the guests would sunbathe or go for a swim, some played tennis, others went for a ride over the hills. Supper would be served at half past eight and afterwards they'd watch a movie; most slept late on Sundays and ate lunch before they left.

One of the guests once offered me a job. He had had too much to drink that night and I suppose it was his way of expressing his gratitude for my services. The following day when he woke up he came directly to find me and asked me to please forget all about it and never mention to the Chief that he had tried to poach me. I assured him I hadn't taken him seriously and wouldn't mention his indiscretion to anyone, least of all the Chief. He was very grateful.

Three weddings in the summer of 1928, I see I've written in my diary, two costume balls, four birthdays, two concerts . . . I see also that this was the summer when the Chief ordered us to move the oak which used to stand right in front of the main building. He bumped his head on the lowest branch when coming out of the house one day and his hat was knocked off. Although he didn't hurt himself, he told me to get in touch with the head gardener and have the tree moved ten feet. Each foot cost a thousand dollars. He didn't care.

This is my world, Elisabet, and I admit that I was dazzled by it. At first I suppose I felt the way I did when I arrived in Copenhagen and discovered that I could leave the past behind. When I'm trying to assuage my conscience I tell myself that this wanderlust is the sign of a born traveler, this eternal longing to be free. I remind myself that I'm descended from a long line of seafarers; that I couldn't wait to leave home when I was a boy.

When I'm depressed I see how pathetic an excuse this is.

I know you won't be surprised to learn that I try to perform my duties conscientiously. As you'll understand, I'm not writing this to boast—who would have thought that I'd ever become a servant again? But I devote myself to my job and often manage to lose myself in the day's business, because there is plenty to do here and the Chief depends on me.

The nights are hardest, when silence surrounds me and there's nothing to deflect the memories. I dread the quiet evenings and try to draw out my chores, sitting up late preparing for the next day, writing myself endless notes or adding to the shopping list, which I always carry, making yet another trip to the pantry to be sure we haven't run out of something that I forgot to put on my list.

The Chief usually stays up late, and I'm happiest when he needs me. He often calls me after midnight, and that's a relief because then I know I'll have something to occupy me for a while. I think he realizes I don't see it as an imposition.

Yes, I perform my duties conscientiously, and if you were like most people you would probably smirk if I described to you the menial jobs that I believe I can perform better than anyone else.

But you were never the vengeful type, never tried to get even with those who had hurt you. That forbearance, where does it come from? Why wouldn't you berate me, take pleasure in seeing me trapped in a web of my own making? Because that would make me feel better. One word from your lips, one word that stung me to the core, and I'd finally have some peace.

But I know you'd be incapable of such behavior. You would consider it vulgar.

Last spring there was a plague of insects here on the hill. At twilight the building was filled with them, starting with the entrance hall, as if they were respectable visitors paying us a house call. They settled on the dinner service and serving dishes, on bars of soap and flower arrangements; every morning they lay dead on all the windowsills, delaying the morning chores. They didn't even let up at night, buzzing in the darkness and keeping everyone awake, the Chief most of all. They would settle on his face and a couple even tried to climb up his nose.

I tried to remember how I had got rid of the flies in our house in Reykjavik but couldn't immediately recall. We had just moved in when the plague hit us; I clearly remember when it reached its peak. It was one evening in June; you were playing Mozart in the living room, you and your friends in the quartet, a woman whose name I forget—skinny, with a long nose—and two young men, one of them in love with you, though you didn't realize. You all invited friends and relatives; people who shared the habit of talking down to me about the "Maestro," as you all called the great composer. Chairs had been set out in the middle of the room; I sat at the back, a guest in my own home. Everyone but you wore a pious expression; you were smiling, your thoughts far away. I shifted in my seat, crossed and recrossed my legs, looked out the window. Then the flies came to my rescue. It was as if the room filled in an instant; the guests began to flap at them, first discreetly, then violently, as if warding off an attack. Your quartet persisted in playing longer than I expected, you longest of all. Finally the gathering broke up. It wasn't until the last person had fled that I set about trying to get rid of the flies.

But now I couldn't remember any longer what tricks I had used. I looked for advice in some old books that I'd found in the Chief's library. Some of what I dug up was interesting in its way, but nothing really worked until I began to experiment myself, from memory. My tactics may not have been particularly scientific, but eventually I stumbled upon a solution that worked. I put half a teaspoon of ground pepper in a shallow bowl along with one teaspoon of soft brown sugar and a tablespoon of cream. I mixed them thoroughly, then put the bowl under the living room window. I changed the mixture daily. After two days the flies were gone.

It was the Chief himself who suggested I write down this tip, along with others which might be useful for the staff here on the hill. This has been a welcome diversion, a way of making time pass more quickly in the evenings and pinning down my thoughts so they don't stray as far off as usual. I've almost finished one exercise book, having written sixty-four tips in it, some quite clever, though I say so myself. But I've plenty more to write, in reality I've only begun. I started indoors, describing things like how best to look after furniture made from mahogany and other types of hardwood, how to get grease stains out of tablecloths, how to polish silver properly, how to clean teapots and coffee mills. I've tried to categorize my thoughts as best I can, so they'll be useful to as many people as possible and are easy to follow, though I reckon I could do better in this respect.

So that's how I kill time in the evenings and early in the mornings when the Chief and Miss Davies are away. As I told you, I've also started picking up a pencil every now and then to sketch the birds here on the hill and down by the sea; sometimes I go down to the shore and sit on a rock with a little sketch pad. Though I'm still rusty, there's no doubt I'm making progress with every week that passes. Next I'm going to try a hawk. And one day I might even have a go at a condor.

The other day the Chief asked me what I was up to. He was taking his evening stroll around the house with his dachshund, Helena, in tow, and put his head round my door. Perhaps he thought he'd find the corpse of a bird on my desk; the dog had been drawn by the smell a few days earlier, when I was attempting the bluebird. I told him I was jotting down my tips, as he had suggested. He asked to see them when I had finished because, who knows, it might be something for the readers of his papers. "We'll see," I said to him. I was thinking that there was plenty that would come in handy for the general public, though I'd have to adjust quite a few things which might seem pretty strange to those who aren't familiar with the ways of rich men's households. I even got quite excited about the prospect of doing this until the Chief said: "We'll give you a byline. We can call the column 'The Butler Suggests,' or something along those lines. You think about it, Christian. It could work. People always want to upgrade their standard of living. Whether they can afford to or not." I was silent. I hope he's forgotten about this idea by now. If he brings it up again, I'll have to tell him I've given up on the whole thing.

So here I am in the dusk, writing in an exercise book about how best to set a table. "*You, Kristjan?*" I hear you say. But I know you won't take pleasure in the fact. You'll just pity me.

They stood before him, three of them, their faces revealing nervous anticipation. It was two o'clock. There was no one else in the staff dining room; most of the household were busy preparing for the ball that evening. He wanted to speak to them in private and so asked them to step aside. The girl jumped when the bell tolled in the tower above them, then smiled shyly and looked down. She had started work a week before and was still unaccustomed. The boys had shiny shoes and slicked-back hair. They were new, as well. There was a clashing of pots and pans from the kitchen but it was muffled and didn't disturb them.

"House rules," he said.

They looked up.

"Three simple rules that the Chief's guests must observe."

Suddenly noticing that someone had forgotten to clean one corner of the table after lunch, he went over to the sink, fetched a wet cloth, wiped down the table, then took it back to the sink and wrung it out before turning back to them.

"Rule one: no drunkenness. You're to watch the guests and let me know the moment you think someone has had too much liquor. Regardless of who it is or what they say.

"Rule two: no bad language or off-color jokes. If the first rule is observed, there's generally no need to worry about people's behavior. Again, you let me know as soon as you believe this rule is being broken.

"Are you with me?"

They nodded.

"Rule three: no sexual intercourse between unmarried couples."

He was about to continue, then fell silent for a moment. They waited.

"No sexual intercourse between unmarried couples," he repeated.

One of the boys, a footman, tried to hide a smile.

"How can we keep a check on that?" he asked.

Kristjan cleared his throat.

"A man and a woman do not sleep in the same room unless they are married. This is a rule. . . . Coming and going between bedrooms is not tolerated . . ." He hesitated. "It's prohibited," he added. "That's a rule, too. Those who break it are sent home the next morning."

Silence. They glanced at one another.

"Three simple rules. Do you trust yourselves to remember them?"

They nodded.

"Good. Then there's no need to keep you."

He went to the door and opened it, showing them out with his eyes.

The inquisitive footman stopped in the doorway.

"May I ask one question?"

The others stopped as well and waited to see what would happen.

"Are the Chief and Miss Davies married, then? Or is it true that he has a wife and family living on the East Coast? Just so we know if we're asked."

Kristjan hesitated a moment.

"You won't be asked," he said after a short silence. "Now go and try to make yourselves useful."

The apple had tumbled out of the pig's jaws and rolled over the port-marinated pears surrounding it, off the silver dish and past the long fork and newly sharpened carving knife. It had come to a halt in the middle of the table as if it had lost heart for a longer journey, yet it didn't seem to feel self-conscious alone in the vast white expanse. The caramel glaze had begun to crack and its wake could be traced in a straight line across the starched table-cloth. The pig stared after it with empty eyes.

It was the evening of the Chief's costume ball. He had invited between sixty and seventy guests, most from Hollywood but also a handful of his own employees—editors and reporters—as well as the odd businessman. Most of the guests had already arrived and were now standing in their rooms before the mirror as they slipped into their costumes—heroes from past centuries, knights, cowboys and popes, clowns and courtesans, queens and nuns.

Kristjan heard a car in the distance and raised a hand to shield his eyes from the late-afternoon glare; the sun hung low in the sky over the ocean and flashed on the black limousine as it crawled up the winding drive.

Reaching into his pocket, he fetched the guest list and peered at it. He reckoned he could guess who was arriving—friends of Miss Davies from Los Angeles, Miss Bette Davis with a director and two other actresses.

"They must have been held up on the way," he said to himself.

Without waiting any longer he turned on his heels and continued his patrol of the buildings.

In the orchard nearest the main building a long trestle table had been set up in a quiet clearing. Pergolas led to the clearing, lined with lamps and torches which would be lit once darkness fell. By the swimming pool a tent was being erected, white with a blue ceiling studded with stars. Wax statues of violin players and a priest with a mouth organ stood side by side outside the tent. Kristjan wiped some bird droppings off the priest's shoulder. He thought he seemed oddly out of place.

He noticed the apple on the table as soon as he looked into the tent. Reacting quickly, he asked someone to fetch the chef and his assistant to repair the table ornaments, ordering two waiters to bring a new cloth. He impressed upon them the importance of keeping their eyes open.

"You're lucky it was me and not the Chief who noticed this," he told them.

In the kitchen, quails, ducks, and pheasants turned on spits over hot coals while outside men were shoveling bundles of wood into a stone-built oven and preparing buffalo joints for roasting. The wood had begun to smoke. Kristjan's gaze inadvertently followed the smoke as it curled out into the quiet afternoon, then he got a grip on himself and continued his patrol before his thoughts could follow it and lose themselves yet again in the stillness.

There was a sweet smell in the air. In the morning two kitchen maids had gone down the hill to pick fruit from the orchard—pineapples and pears, oranges, bananas, and nuts. They had washed the fruit, placed them in rows on trays, and arranged them meticulously in numerous bowls. Kristjan paused in the kitchen to check that they had performed their task properly, before reminding the stand-in chef yet again that the Chief liked his meat rare.

An hour later the guests were gathered in the Assembly Room. Kristjan alerted the Chief and Miss Davies when everyone was present. They took the elevator together from their adjoining bedrooms and entered through the concealed door in the paneled wall, like gods, with a calm, distant look in their eyes. They stood motionless side by side until their guests became aware of them. A murmur passed through the crowd, then voices were lowered, people looked up from their chessboards or jigsaw puzzles; those who were visiting for the first time glanced around in the hope of picking up clues on how to behave. But there was no need for guidance because after a few seconds Miss Davies came to life like a wax doll touched by a magic wand. Her face broadened in a smile as she released the Chief's hand and vanished into the crowd that welcomed her with hugs and kisses. David Niven, dressed as a pickpocket. Bette Davis with a beard. Carole Lombard in a Tyrolean outfit. These were her friends and they adored her.

The Chief, meanwhile, turned aside to check his messages on the Teletype machine.

Kristjan thought Hearst didn't seem right that evening. There had been no warning earlier in the day but now he saw that something was wrong. He was sure it wasn't business that worried him, because the Chief never let it show when times were tough. "Miss Davies," he muttered to himself, and determined to keep a close eye on her during the evening.

He noticed that a guest at the other side of the room looked rather the worse for wear and nudged one of the footmen, indicating that he was not to fill the man's glass again. According to the Chief's rules, the guests were not permitted more than two glasses of spirits before dinner or three glasses of wine. Kristjan knew from experience that it could be difficult to keep track of consumption among so many people, particularly at the beginning of a party when the guests were drinking on empty stomachs. Some were weary from their journey but the excitement always overcame them and then they forgot how much they had consumed. He was in no doubt about whom the Chief would hold accountable if anyone got drunk. Especially Miss Davies. He would be a long time forgetting the Chief's eyes at the dinner table when she had passed out once in her chair opposite him. Yet no one had seen her take a drink all evening; no one had seen her touch anything but water. She had hidden a flask of gin in her handbag and drunk from it when no one was looking.

The guests filed out one by one. They were greeted by the evening sun, pale and timid on the ground but more cheerful in the branches of the trees, and lively on the streams and fountains. The chef adjusted his hat and wielded his carving knife on the first pig. There were nine more waiting their turn.

The Chief remained inside with a few of his guests; he was dressed as a woodcutter in brown breeches and a green jerkin with gilt buttons. On his head a feather bounced in a flat cap of green velour. Apparently it was tight since he kept taking it off and rubbing his forehead. He surveyed the room ceaselessly but couldn't see Miss Davies. Three of his guests, middle-aged men whom Kristjan knew to be in the newspaper business, stood around him, talking away obliviously as he scanned the room.

Could she have gone outside?

The dusk was deepening in the gardens, the shadows of the trees lengthening. Kristjan paused for a moment on his way to the tent to watch the lighting of the lamps. Generally a sense of calm flooded over him at this time of day, but now he was on edge and had no time to savor the view or the twilight spreading over the mountainsides and the plain below. In the spring the dusk approached like silent veils of rain, but in winter it wore a gray gown. With the dusk he sensed her presence, why he didn't know.

"Klara," he'd say, when he felt her coming closer. "Are you sleepwalking again?"

Just as he was about to continue on his rounds, someone nudged him. He jumped and turned sharply. Miss Davies smiled at him.

"My glass . . . fill it up, dear."

"You know . . ."

"Just a teeny bit."

". . . I can't."

The smile lingered on her lips but the tone of her voice changed.

"Come on, quick. Fill up my glass."

"I'm sorry."

"Don't be like that. Come on."

Silence.

"Fill my glass, I say."

"The Chief . . ."

She didn't raise her voice but it quivered as if someone had plucked an overtaut string.

"To hell with him. He doesn't know what I've been through. I can't do it again. It gets worse every time."

He didn't know what she was referring to. She had begun to shake and was on the verge of tears.

"Is there something I can do?" he asked.

"Yes, fill my glass," she begged. "Please just fill my glass . . ."

He took her arm.

"Come on," he coaxed. "You'll feel better when you've had something to eat. The guests are waiting."

He led her to the main building, out of the half-dusk and mist and towards the twinkling lights. The noise of the party reached them, roars of laughter and the clinking of cutlery and glass; she gripped his arm tight, gradually loosening her hold as she managed to suppress her sobs.

Was he trying to console her when he said all of a sudden: "Do you remember when Mr. Valentino taught you how to dance the tango right here in the garden?" He didn't know; maybe he just meant to comfort himself. But whatever his reason, she said without looking at him: "Yes, it was awful. Even when I was happy, I couldn't dance."

When they had climbed up to the terrace nearest the house, the Chief came towards them. She straightened up, touched anew by the magic wand, and said with a smile:

"There you are, dear."

Kristjan hurried away, past the musicians who had begun to play in front of a statue of the Three Graces, and the guests who were dancing on the terrace, looking neither to right nor left but quickening his pace until he reached the doorway of the tent. There he stopped, at last to catch his breath and wipe the pearls of sweat from his brow. Pursuing him into the tent, the music would have seemed sweet and uplifting under different circumstances—"I only have eyes for you . . ."

There was hardly anything left of the pig on the long trestle table but the apple was still gripped in its jaw. When the waiters replaced it with a slightly smaller pig, Kristjan made sure they put parsley eyelashes and cranberry eyes where the pig's own eyes had once been.

The guests had gone to bed.

I was the only one left downstairs; the staff had finally retired to their rooms, the kitchen maids last of all. I had turned off all the lights and was making a last tour of the ground-floor rooms to make sure that all the candles had been blown out and no cigarettes had been left smoldering. The logs had burned down in the great hearth in the assembly room, though the embers still sent up the occasional spark. Through the window I saw that a lamp was still shining in Casa del Mar. I felt better knowing that someone else was still awake. I don't know why.

All the lights were out, yet it was bright where I stood in the middle of the reception room. The moon was now high in the sky and laid a long strip of light across the mirror-like ocean, up the hillside, across the floor—to my feet. I walked towards it, opening the terrace door. Everything was quiet. I hoped the antelope, leopard, and puma would be able to sleep tonight. I didn't like them being locked up in cages in this place; they didn't belong here. None of them belonged here.

The air still held the fragrance of woodsmoke and the pungent smell of pine, which I never notice except in the evenings. A reverberation came and went, a distant echo which I tried to concentrate on. But the evening's songs got in the way—"I don't know if it's cloudy or bright, 'cause I only have eyes for you . . ." I stepped inadvertently backwards, first two steps, then another. The moonlight pursued me, surrounded me, as if I were standing in shallow water. I looked down and stared at my feet for a while, the refrain in my ears slowly changing, the evening's songs falling silent and the echo growing clearer in my mind.

I was walking in through the door of our house in Eyrarbakki. It was after midnight, the servants had gone to bed, little Einar was long since fast asleep. You were sitting in your chair in the living room, just finishing breast-feeding Maria. You looked up and smiled when I came in; I put down my suitcases and quietly removed my coat and hung it up. You slipped your nipple from her mouth. She was asleep, so you got up and laid her in her cradle before coming over to me. I had just returned from a month in Denmark. I put my arms round you in the middle of the room and pulled you against me, neither of us saying a word. All of a sudden you began to hum. I recognized the tune immediately— "Bei Männern," from *The Magic Flute*—you used to play it so often when we first met. I began to move to the rhythm and you followed. I pressed you against me, couldn't let you go, didn't want to let you go. There was a lantern burning on top of a cupboard, shedding a faint light.

I began to dance in the moonlit reception room. How silly I must have looked! But I felt as if you were with me. It was as if nothing had changed, everything was as it had been before I lost my way. Because that's what happened. I lost my way. But now, for a moment, I had found my way back and I shut my eyes and held on tight to your memory. You hadn't buttoned up your blouse after feeding Maria and I undid it even further as we swayed around the room. Your breasts were hot and soft and I took your nipple into my mouth, gently because I knew it was still sore from the baby. You had stopped humming now but we continued to dance.

I didn't know that she had come down and started to dance with me. I wasn't aware of her, I was so far away, your breath soothing against my cheek. The moonlight lapped the floor under our feet; we undulated as if dancing in water.

"Christian," she whispered.

I came to with a jolt.

"Fetch a drop of gin for me. Booth's. Quickly, so we can keep going."

The silence was broken. I thought I heard the puma snarling lower down the hill.

"What's the matter, Christian?"

"I'm sorry," I said. "I'm sorry . . ."

I fetched the gin bottle from the locked cupboard and a glass on a tray. I spilled the liquor outside the glass and had difficulty cleaning up after myself.

"Christian . . ."

Leaving her behind in the middle of the room, I hurried away, trying to say good night but unable to get the words out.

My fingers smelled of gin. I noticed it when I locked the door to my room and buried my face in my hands. I had done wrong, yet again.

I harm everyone I care for.

When he awoke and looked outside he thought at first that there had been a frost during the night. It was dawn; a veil of fog unfurled from the sea and rolled up over the sand dunes that lined the shore and the meadows which seemed gray with rime in the early-morning light. The remnants of a dream still echoed in his head so he couldn't immediately remember where he was. When he finally got his bearings, it occurred to him that it was dew, not frost, that bowed the grasses. He moved slowly, tugging a warm sweater over his head before opening the window and inhaling the chill air.

He heated himself water for tea in the silent kitchen. The Chief and Miss Davies had been away for a week; he didn't know when to expect them back. The uncertainty troubled him.

The Chief had abruptly been called away. His advisers had sent a telegram an hour before the costume ball, announcing their arrival the following day. Kristjan brought it immediately to Hearst, who hardly looked at it.

They wasted no time. It was just past ten when their car appeared at the bottom of the hill; they had left Los Angeles in the middle of the night. Kristjan brought them coffee while they waited in the billiards room. They seemed on edge. The Chief kept them waiting nearly an hour. Miss Davies was still asleep; some of the weekend guests were up, having breakfast on the terrace.

He was wearing a silk robe when he finally came downstairs, holding a copy of one of his newspapers—the *San Francisco Examiner,* Kristjan concluded after a quick glance. Instead of coming directly into the room, he paused in the doorway and regarded them in silence.

"Christian," he said after a moment, "could you bring me some fruit juice?"

Without waiting for his butler to move out of earshot, he addressed his visitors:

"I thought we hired Walter Winchell to write a gossip column about actors and entertainers. Since when did he become our expert on the Spanish Civil War?"

He flung the paper onto the table in front of his advisers. Kristjan closed the door behind him.

In the kitchen he prepared the Chief's morning drink, a mixture of carrot and orange juice. A bee had wandered in through a gap in the window and was buzzing from one pane to the next. Kristjan watched it for a while, then opened the window a crack and let it out.

He could hear the Chief's voice out in the passage as he approached the billiards room:

"It's none of our business if Fascists and Communists are killing each other in Spain. We don't support either side. I thought everyone knew that. At least the people on our payroll. Then I open my own paper and read this nonsense! Walter Winchell urging the nation to go to war in Spain! Walter Winchell, who was hired to keep our readers informed about who's feuding with whom in Hollywood and who's marrying whom on Broadway. Walter Winchell of all people . . ."

He frowned heavily at his guests, adding, after a moment's pause:

"And on top of that he has totally neglected to write about Miss Davies recently. Totally neglected her . . . Perhaps he should be looking for another job."

Kristjan handed the Chief his glass of fruit juice. The Chief beckoned him to stay. There were three of them. Kristjan knew Jack Neylan by name but he'd never seen the other two before, both men of around thirty. They were obviously nervous and their eyes flickered to Neylan in the hope that he would break the silence and state their case quickly. The Chief drank his juice slowly.

"We're in trouble, Chief," said Neylan at last. "It's worse than before."

It wasn't the first time Kristjan had heard the Chief's advisers complaining about his spending, and urging him to abandon his endless purchasing of works of art and antiques.

"Even if it was just for a few months," he remembered Neylan saying over and over again one evening in New York.

The Chief normally listened patiently but let their talk and their worries wash over him, changing the subject and ending with: "You'll take care of this for me. Shouldn't be a problem."

Kristjan had also heard Neylan say that the Depression had hit the Chief's companies so hard that some of his papers and magazines were now struggling. Circulation had dropped in Los Angeles, San Francisco, Chicago, and Boston, and in addition papers like the *New York American,* the *Evening Journal,* and the *Sunday American* had all lost readers during the last four years. He knew, too, that the Chief had financed the buildings on the hill and the purchase of a castle in Wales and a mansion on Long Island with loans that he sustained by issuing debt and shares in his companies before taking out new loans to pay off the old ones. The antiques and works of art were paid for in the same way, that is to say when Hearst remembered. It had not escaped Kristjan that he had debts all over the place.

Yet he had never thought it would come to this and was stunned when Neylan described why the profit from the Chief's business ventures was not sufficient to cover either the interest on his loans or to pay the dividends on the shares. He said it had come to the point where the banks were not only refusing to refinance their outstanding loans but also demanding that he pay them off.

The morning sunshine filtered in through the corner window, onto the billiards table, next to which the Chief stood. With his forefinger he slowly and deliberately traced the sunlight, his thoughts elsewhere. Finally his finger came to a halt. Without lifting it, he looked over towards the window.

"You must come with us to New York as quickly as you can," said Neylan. "Preferably today or tomorrow. We have to start negotiating with the banks."

The Chief continued to stare at the sunlight.

"What do we need to give them to make them happy?"

"A million dollars immediately. And that's before we start selling assets."

He removed his finger from the table.

"Sell assets? Out of the question."

"We can't avoid it any longer. We can't even scrape together a million dollars without sacrificing some assets."

They didn't notice when she entered the room. She stood in the doorway behind Kristjan. He sensed her presence on the nape of his neck.

"I want you to sell everything I own," she said, clearly taking them aback. "That ought to cover it."

She departed as silently as she had arrived. The Chief left in pursuit. His advisers looked at one another, then hastily took their leave as well.

Later that day the Chief and Miss Davies drove to Los Angeles, where they took the *Super Chief* to New York. There was not a breath of wind as they disappeared down the hill, and the dust cloud thrown up in their wake hung in the air like a memorial long after they had gone.

That was a week ago. How time flies, he said to himself as the kettle whistled to let him know that the water had boiled. He moved slowly, rubbing his hands together over the steaming cup to warm them. It was an unusually cold morning and the grass was still wet with dew, no longer gray but yellow where the pale rays of the sun touched it, blue in the shade. He was the only one up; there were fewer staff in residence than usual. The day after the Chief left for New York, Kristjan had informed the temporary staff that they would not be required for the next few weeks.

The tea warmed him. When he had finished it, and the slice of bread he had buttered for himself, he meant to go round behind the main building to the workmen's huts. He had promised to help them take the hay to the stables and was looking forward to sitting on the back of the truck with the pitchforks as they drove along the dirt tracks to the barn. He was looking forward to the sweet smell of dried grass, and to seeing the whites of the horses' eyes as they watched him fork the hay down from the truck. And most of all he was looking forward to the physical exertion of a long, sweaty day laboring under the sun.

He opened the door and stepped slowly out into the shimmering morning, cautiously, as if not to disturb an unaccustomed peace of mind. He closed the door quietly, leaving the empty rooms behind.

I don't have much to tell you tonight. Don't take my words to mean that I hadn't been wondering what I should write to you when I finally sat down at my desk this evening. But for some reason I couldn't summon up the energy to reach for the pen and unscrew the cap. *Pen,* I write, but, to be more accurate, it's the pen you gave me when I turned thirty. I've carried it with me ever since. I had fetched a snow-white sheet of paper and placed it in the center of the desk, adjusted its position a couple of times and brushed off some pollen that had blown in the window when suddenly I was overcome and all the words seemed to have lost their meaning. It was as if the sun had gone behind a cloud and a shadow had fallen across my mind. At that moment it seemed to me that everything I'd written to you over the past few months was empty and pointless.

I sat as if paralyzed in my chair, for this melancholy had struck without warning. Ever since this morning I had been looking forward to telling you about the mouse I found in a plant pot down in the living room the day before yesterday; all of a sudden it seemed so strangely dear to me. I dug a little hole in the garden and covered it with some bits of twig and leaves to make it cozy. I was going to describe to you how terrified it was when I took it out of the plant pot, because Helena had found it and was barking loudly and shoving her snout at it. How its little heart pounded as I carried it outside; it quivered in my hands but didn't try to struggle, and I wondered whether it could sense—or, rather, whether it could sense in *me*—that I wouldn't do it any harm. I had even begun to convince myself that I'd managed to communicate through my hands alone that I wished it well and would take care of it.

I dug the hole in the flower bed outside Casa del Monte. It looked as if the wind was going to pick up during the evening, so I found a place between two stones where I knew it would be safe. During the night it began to rain, the branches of the palm tree outside my window lashed the house, and the rain battered the windowpanes. I couldn't sleep, so I dressed and went down to the kitchen, stuck a piece of cheese in my pocket, and went outside. I was drenched within seconds as I hurried down the path. I was worried that the mouse might be out in the storm, so I was mightily relieved when I lifted the leaf from the hole.

It was as if it knew I would come back. I took care not to shine the flashlight I'd brought with me in its eyes, but I couldn't help noticing that its gaze showed unconditional trust.

I can't explain the moment of happiness I experienced as I knelt there beside the hole in the darkness. Why a tiny mouse should have such an effect on me . . . It ate the cheese out of my hand and didn't move even though I stroked its back over and over. Thunder shook the sky and lightning tore it apart but the mouse remained calm under my finger.

The following morning the sky was cloudless and the air smelled sweet after the rain. I knew even before I reached the hole that the mouse had gone.

That's what I meant to write to you when I sat down in my chair this evening. I hadn't read anything into these events but I was looking forward to telling you about them. The sheet of paper waited, blank and snowy, before me, but suddenly I was snatched away, my fingers lost their grip on the pen, and I didn't come to myself until the cap fell to the floor with a click.

I stood up and went over to the window. Before I knew it I had begun to breathe on the glass like I used to as a boy. A circular patch of mist formed; I put out my finger and drew a little bird in it. A few seconds later it was gone.

She sat up in bed and stretched a slender finger towards the window by her head. A sudden shiver ran through her when its tip touched the icy pane, but instead of withdrawing her hand, she wiped the mist from the glass and put the wet finger into her mouth. The room was warming up; she had been asleep when the maid came in and lit the stove. All was quiet and she lay back, pulling the down comforter up to her chin, turning her head so that she could see out of the window, and waiting as she did as a child for a bird to fly past. She guessed it would be a tern—no, a sandpiper—and lay still to see if she was right.

She had arrived home in Eyrarbakki yesterday morning after being abroad for a year and a half, having left in the fall of 1907. Her father came down to the jetty to meet her, while the maid, Katrin, hung back, half-hidden, peeping shyly now and then from behind a stack of empty barrels. She had been with the family since Elisabet was a small child and had missed her every day that she was away.

She thought her father had aged during her absence. His cheeks were wet when he hugged her at the foot of the gangplank, his hands cold and the look in his eyes more distant than before, as if some part of him had taken its leave.

"My sunbeam," he kept saying. "My sunbeam has come home."

She was home, yet her mind roamed ceaselessly. She smiled absentmindedly when Kristjan appeared in her thoughts, brushed the hair off her brow and stood still, remembering every detail of his face.

Wood crackled in the stove. The silence in the house seemed more marked after the dancing yesterday. It was heavier, more uncompromising than usual, as if making sure that the echo of the party would not dispel it. The celebration had gone on past midnight; Elisabet was tired after her journey but her father couldn't contain his joy and gave the same speech three times, the last time standing on the long dining-room table, breaking off only when he lost his footing.

"And now my sunbeam has come home and it's as if a light has been brought into the house and now everything will be bright and beautiful and good. Lisa, my dear, come here."

"Father . . ."

"Now, now, come to your old man because I'm going to tell our guests—now I'm going to announce to our guests—that you're engaged."

The guests cheered with excitement.

"Don't be cross with me, Lisa dear, I just couldn't wait."

"Who's the lucky man?" called out Paulsen the pharmacist.

"Kristjan Benediktsson, he's called, from the West Fjords, a fine lad. Fine lad, I say. They met in Copenhagen."

"When you weren't looking!"

"Hey, Paulsen, I'll get you for that, you rascal!"

And then she was hugged and kissed.

"Dear Elisabet, my darling girl, who are his parents?" . . . "When's the wedding?" . . . "Is he still in Copenhagen?" . . . "When's he coming over?"

Her father flung his arms round his friend Paulsen and, waving to the harmonica player to strike up a tune, danced with him across the room.

The party guests linked hands and formed a ring in the living room. Placing her in the middle, they surged up to her and away again by turns. She closed her eyes, imagining he was there with her, and danced alone, or rather floated until her father broke out of the ring and took her in his arms.

The house seemed weary after the joyful night. Even the chimes of the dining room clock seemed slower than usual. But her room had warmed up and there was a comforting crackling sound from the stove; when she was small she used to believe she could understand the words it whispered to her as she was dropping off to sleep. It never failed to tell her what she wanted to hear.

A black house with open sea to the south, behind it the moors and bleak open spaces, around it huts, outbuildings, and the fishermen's bunkhouse. Eyes in the window upstairs and a clock striking in the dining room below; otherwise silence. There was no one about, the gravel path along the shore was empty; there was no movement except when the wind flattened the pale grasses by the path.

A sandpiper flew by.

For centuries, Eyrarbakki, a small village thirty miles from Reykjavik, had been the main port and trading center for the southern part of the country. Elisabet's father ran both the store and the fishing boats that operated from the harbor; Iceland belonged to the Danish crown and he held his agency direct from the king. He'd even persuaded Queen Louise of Denmark, wife of King Christian IX, to paint the altarpiece in the church that he'd had built in 1890. After a drop too much, he used to say that he'd done this in order to get an accurate picture of the Savior, for surely royalty must be better acquainted with Him than the great unwashed proletariat.

It was late in April that the first ships of spring arrived at Eyrarbakki, impressive vessels, two-masted schooners of eighty to a hundred tons, seldom crewed by fewer than six men. Lighters plied back and forth from their anchorage, ferrying coal, salt, and grain to shore. Rye was usually carried in the hold under the loose goods, while wheat and barley were shipped in sacks. Iron for horseshoes, roofing iron, and nails were packed in crates, as was cloth. Planks and boards were shipped separately. Floorboards and panels were hand-planed at her father's workshop between the store and the warehouses where the coffee was kept alongside sugar and raw spirits. The alcohol was thinned with rainwater from the store roof before being poured into hogsheads with their three-way faucets; one for bottles, another for casks, and the third for barrels. One evening when her father visited the store after a drop too much, he mistook one of the hogsheads in the shadowy corner for an ox. Running home, he fetched a rifle, woke one of the workmen, and asked him to come with him. As they crashed through the door and rushed inside, he fired off a shot at the hogshead. After that, the hogsheads were known as ox-heads.

Landing the cargo took up to a week, and then, in turn, work began on ferrying wool, saltfish, and cod-liver oil out to the ships. The wool was transported to Eyrarbakki by trains of packhorses, and the farmers often had to camp by the shop wall for two to three days before their turn came to be served.

She liked the smell of the horses and opened the window by the piano to let it into the room. The music carried out into the stillness and the farmers edged nearer to listen. They caught a glimpse of a pale cheek in the window, through gauzy white curtains decorated with yellow flowers and butterflies flitting among them. Some of the farmers sat on the garden wall, silently chewing long-stemmed grass, putting their heads together now and then to whisper, so they wouldn't drown out the rippling notes.

Sometimes she looked up, yet they sensed she wasn't looking at them but out over the bay at the white sails which the mild wind flapped occasionally as if to amuse itself. For a brief moment— then she would look down again, and the long, slender fingers would continue to send their songs out into the quiet afternoon.

Her father had forbidden her to go out alone while the ships were anchored in the bay. Enjoying the sea and shore from the parlor window, she didn't mind, she didn't particularly want to go out. She knew the reason for this ban, though she never told him that she knew. She had been about ten when it happened.

She never knew the girl's name. She was from the southwest, a fisherman's daughter. It was her second summer loading cargo at Eyrarbakki. She had been stacking saltfish in the hold during the day and the men had been friendly and said something to her that she didn't understand, so she just smiled because they had smiled at her. They appeared to be only a few years older than she was, of average height, one dark, the other fair.

Most of the day had been overcast and still but in the evening the wind rose and it rained. She had finished her dinner and was on her way to the bunkhouse when she met them. They smiled. This time she didn't smile back because something in their manner made her uneasy. They had been drinking. The fair one took a swig and offered her the bottle. She shook her head and tried to slip past them, along the path by the shore, past the pump-house. It was at that point that they seized her arm and dragged her inside.

Later that evening when she sat in Elisabet's father's office she couldn't for the life of her remember which of them had grabbed her first. She had been weeping but now sat silently, staring ahead with empty eyes. Her sister spoke for her and described the incident. She was a year or two older, and it had been her decision to come to the boss for help.

He sat in his office chair, at first staring out of the window at the fog hovering along the shore and hiding the ships and the breakwater beyond them. It was only when he lowered his head that he realized his hands were clenched under the desk, the knuckles white. He loosened his grip.

Elisabet was awakened by the commotion. She got out of bed and went downstairs in a white nightdress which covered her thin body down to her ankles. The office door was open a crack; she followed the sound, stopped outside.

She saw her father stand up, go to the girl, and get down on his knees with difficulty before her, touching her hand gently. She could see his face, but only the back of the girl's head. Her hair was tied in a bun. She had obviously washed up before coming to see him.

"Could you describe them for me, dear?" she heard her father say. The girl nodded but remained silent. Her father waited, shifting his weight from left leg to right.

"There, there, dear," he said at last and took her hand.

She started to sob but then spoke. She remembered the cold, damp, mossy walls, the lapping of the waves in the fog, the rocks on the shore which could be glimpsed from the pump-house door before the fog hid them again. She remembered the singing of the water, the taste of blood in her mouth. And her feet making wet marks in the grass when she finally stumbled home.

Later that night, when her father had summoned the ship's captain and the men had been brought ashore, Elisabet put on a blue cape and went outside. The wind had dropped. In the east there was a hint of red between the clouds. The sea was silent. She walked lightly down the path by the shore, not stopping until she came to the bunkhouse where the girl was staying.

The girl's eyes were open, the others slept. When she reached the girl she drew from her pocket the locket that she had brought with her. It had been her mother's; there was a picture of a meadowsweet inside. She leaned down to the girl and laid it round her neck. Then slipped out.

The next day the girl told her sister that an angel had visited her in the night.

On the way home Elisabet stopped by the pump-house and went inside. Blue light filtered through a slit in the roof; she put out her hand so that the ray of light illuminated it, then closed her fist. The cold silence was broken only by the clear, pure voice of the water. Elisabet listened. When she was convinced that its song hadn't changed, she went back out into the dawn light and headed for home.

She stood by the kitchen fire, warming herself. A platter on the table beside her held two freshly caught haddock, their scales glistening. She wished she could follow the advice of Mrs. Andersen, whom she had lodged with in Copenhagen, and fillet and fry them with mushrooms and parsley, but she didn't know how. She moved closer to the flames, stretching out her hands and listening in silence to the crackling fire.

She didn't notice when Katrin crept in. Katrin had avoided her since she came home, as if shy of her. She stopped in the doorway and coughed. Elisabet turned round and smiled at her, then continued warming herself. She was still chilled after her walk along the shore.

Katrin spoke softly, muttering into her chest:

"Aren't you going to finish embroidering the panel, then?"

"What?"

"The panel you were halfway through when you left for Copenhagen."

Katrin had had meningitis as a child and people who didn't know her well said it showed. Elisabet never thought about it. She and Katrin had always been like family.

Elisabet beckoned her over and shifted so that there was room for both of them in the warmth from the hearth.

"That embroidery with the little castles. And deer and trees."

"Are there deer on it?"

"Big deer. Almost as big as the castles."

Katrin stretched out her hands like Elisabet, though she had been warm all morning. Elisabet took them in her own hands and ran her fingers over them. They were rough.

"Wouldn't *you* like to finish the embroidery?" asked Elisabet.

"Me? No, it's yours."

"You can have it. I'd forgotten all about it."

"Thank you, Lisa. I'm so happy you're back."

Water trickled into the corner sink in a thin, faltering stream. Otherwise, all was quiet. Elisabet noticed a carpenter striding along the path outside, entering the storehouse by the garden wall and emerging with a couple of planks. He looked up at the sky. Life crawled forward. Nothing had changed. Almost nothing.

"Two weeks," said Katrin.

"One week."

"Until you get married."

"Until he comes home."

Each day was like the next, the sea in the morning and the sea in the evening, wood in the stove when she awoke, the piano in the parlor, the wind in the birch scrub and the smell of burning kindling from the store where they smoked sheep's heads. Her father asleep in his chair at the end of the day, a book in his lap, his glasses perched on the tip of his nose, mouth open.

"Lisa?" said Katrin softly.

"Yes?"

"When you're married . . ."

"Yes?"

". . . and your father is dead . . . You know how much I care about him . . ."

It was on the tip of Elisabet's tongue to say that her father was as strong as an ox, though he was getting on. He's still very healthy, she was about to say, but didn't.

". . . then what'll happen to me?"

"Katrin, dear Katrin. Please don't worry. Father's not about to go anywhere, but when it does happen, you'll stay with me. Always. With us."

"Do you think he'll have me? Your husband?"

"Of course."

"I've been so worried."

She leaned against Elisabet, resting her head on her shoulder.

"Tell me about him . . ."

I was just trying to remember what you were wearing the first time we met. I'm sitting in the kitchen, letting my mind wander, having filed the bills away in the drawer and prepared the shopping list for next week. A moment's quiet in the house. Outside on the terrace a squirrel has just climbed down from a tree and scampered across the path with an acorn in its mouth.

It was a cold autumn day and leaves were blowing along the street outside—Skindergade, if I remember right, Universitets Café—and I closed the door for you because you had your hands full of sheet music and had dropped a brown glove as you came in. I remember stooping to pick up the glove and dusting down my white waiter's apron before showing you to a table. You didn't take off your coat, which was brown with a fur collar, because you seemed chilled, but ordered a cup of coffee and a sandwich, asking as I turned away:

"You're not Icelandic, are you?"

Though I'd been looking you over, I'd never have guessed that we were compatriots. There was no telling from your accent that you were Icelandic—your Danish was impeccable—and from your appearance, the brown eyes and dark wavy hair, you might have been from the south—Spain, Italy, Greece. I'd been covertly watching you, lurking by the kitchen door and gazing at the back of your neck and your right cheek when you turned your head to look at the book you'd opened on the table in front of you. It grew dark outside and shortly afterwards the pattering of rain began. When the gray light illuminated your cheek, I felt as if I were looking at a statue.

"You're not Icelandic, are you?"

I was taken aback. I had little contact with the other Icelanders here. Most young men my age had come to study, they were the sons of rich families or scholarship boys. I had nothing in common with them. I was neither and had come to Copenhagen with no firm plans, hoping for the best, empty-handed after earning my passage as a fisherman for almost a year. My family didn't have much, though I never lacked for anything when I was growing up. Yet as I stood in the kitchen doorway I felt I had to make excuses for my situation. Perhaps I should say it differently: I felt I had to invent a suitable explanation to account for my being a waiter. But you didn't ask any questions and it wasn't until later, when I couldn't help myself, that I told you I was studying at the Commercial College in Copenhagen.

I'm still surprised at how inferior I felt when I stood there. I had always found it easy to attract women, but you were different. They were mostly working girls, fun-loving but uneducated— like me. But you, you were from a different world. And yet I found myself falling towards you.

I was only nine when I started working on the boats. I'd begged my father to take me with him when I was younger but my mother wouldn't hear of it. I was always restless, always eager to be on the move. "He's a born fisherman," my uncle used to say, and I was proud. But I never had any aspirations to own a boat myself, I didn't want to have to worry about the responsibility.

When we met, I had just spent several days working on a picture of an eagle. I had paint on my fingers and you asked me what I'd been up to. You seemed interested when I mentioned the birds and asked when I had first started drawing them. I told you how once when I was a boy I had seen an eagle swoop in from the sea and circle over a flock of eider ducks that dived to escape him. I told you how the eagle waited while the ducks popped their heads up for air and then dived again and again. He waited patiently until they tired. Then he dropped, wings aloft, talons driving down, and took one as it dived. As I watched him flapping away down the fjord, I was rooted to the spot. The shadow of his wings on the flat surface of the sea. Death in his talons.

You listened in silence.

I stood by the window in your room, looking out at the empty streets. Saturday morning. Footsteps on the floor upstairs: the neighbors were awake. I had lit the stove but my breath still formed mist in the air after the chill of the night. You got out of bed and joined me. Your fingers were cold when you ran them along the scar on my back. Beginning at the top—with your forefinger, I thought—you traced slowly down my back. Stopped, then continued under my arm and round onto my chest.

"How old were you?"

"I was eight."

You came closer. I felt your breath on my back before your lips touched the scar. The finger continued on its journey. It was as if you were exploring a map and had stopped on the boundary between the familiar and the unknown. You lifted my arm and inserted your head underneath, kissing me on the chest and looking up into my face. I thought I saw curiosity in your eyes.

Once outside, I walked across the street and looked up at your window. You waved to me, wrapped in a white sheet. The wind had picked up and was blowing winter over the city. I wound my scarf round my neck.

Before saying goodbye, I had told you about my studies at the Commercial College. I'd had the story prepared for days, but you never asked. You didn't ask about anything. And that was the worst. I felt as if you were trying to spare my feelings. As if you saw through everything already.

I said I was taking business courses. On Mondays, Thursdays, and Fridays from three till six. I had six months left till I graduated. I was getting on well. I was waiting on tables to make a little extra.

While I was speaking, you sat up in bed and turned towards me. Your breasts were like pears, white and beautiful, the nipples hard in the morning chill. Fingers long and delicate. When you touched me, I was in your power.

Did you know then that this story was a lie? Did you know that I cleaned the classrooms on Mondays, Thursdays, and Fridays? The graduation certificate I brought home to Iceland before we married was a forgery. You had it framed and hung it above my desk in the office at home.

Has completed his studies in Accounting, Commodities, Invoicing, and General Economics with the highest marks.

I had bought the textbooks and studied alone in the library when I'd finished cleaning, but I couldn't afford to attend courses.

I never corrected these lies. By the time I wanted to, it was too late.

When did you find out?

A golden plover awoke in the marshes, flying through the spring night like a black thread through a white blanket.

Had she been awakened by the swish of the bird's wings or was she dreaming? Elisabet climbed out of bed. As she turned the door handle and stepped out onto the landing, the dining-room clock struck three faint chimes. Someone had forgotten to close a window at the end of the hallway. When she shut the window she noticed the fog out in the bay. As she was about to return to her room, she again heard the sound which had awakened her. Unable to work out immediately where it was coming from, she paused and looked alternately down the stairs and along the hallway to the other bedroom wing.

The curtains over the window she had shut were now still, the embroidered carriages awaiting their passengers, the teams hanging their heads in neat rows, their reins slack.

Silence. She waited, and as she did so her eyes fell on the portrait of her mother that hung on the wall by the stairs. Lately she had been wondering whether she had ever missed her. She'd been a child of three when she died, too young for such feelings.

She turned abruptly and headed along to the other wing. The

sound became increasingly clear, though she still couldn't work out what it was—breathing? Rattling? Whispering? She walked towards it with slow, even steps.

When an icy draft swept along the floor, she stopped for a second, as if she had stepped into water. She bent automatically to dry her toes but her fingers encountered nothing but cold.

Am I dreaming, she asked herself?

She hesitated outside her father's bedroom. The door was not closed but stood a little ajar, admitting a thin crack of light which stretched across the floor and up to his bed. She gave the door a light push.

He was moving slowly between her legs, slowly and steadily like the pendulum in the dining-room clock downstairs. "Oh yes," she heard him say, "oh yes." He was wearing a white nightshirt but Katrin's bare arms were pink in the dawn light when she put them round his back.

She pulled the door quietly to and tiptoed swiftly back to her own room. Lying down with eyes closed, she wondered why it was that this sight should not have bothered her in the least.

I came to Iceland a week before the wedding.

The fog lifted suddenly as we approached the south coast. Without warning, the mountains appeared above our heads, a patch of sunshine on their slopes.

It was raining out in the bay, a dense, unremitting drizzle; birds mewed above us.

I didn't feel as if I were coming home. When I left, I was nothing. Now I felt myself shrinking again.

I saw the rivers meandering over the sands and vanishing into the sea, the glaciers beyond them hidden in blue mist. A white ribbon of cloud hung from a black peak by the shore, gilded now and then by the morning sun, but never for long. Except for a green streak here and there among the roots of the mountains, all was white, gray, and black.

Perhaps I hadn't had enough sleep.

The great open spaces before me and the cold silence of the sands awoke no feeling of freedom in my breast. Rather it was as if I were gradually being bound with invisible fetters, until I wanted to scream at the barren wasteland. In Copenhagen I woke a free man in the mornings, sometimes at the side of a girl whom I'd danced with till dawn, at other times alone. Then I'd lie still in bed for a few minutes before getting up, listening to a horse pulling a cart down the cobbled street, the fishmonger across the road bearing the wet, glittering night's catch into his shop, the people downstairs getting out of bed, opening the window onto the street, coughing, saying: "Well, better get moving."

I was part of this life, in the midst of it, and no one doubted my right to be there, no one asked who I was, no one looked askance at me. I smiled at people and they smiled back, some even turned round in the street and said to themselves or their companion: "That was a handsome young man." I was hardworking, with the sense to put money aside; I was the owner of two smart suits, one blue, the other brown, as well as hats, overcoats, three pairs of good shoes, and an umbrella, though I used it rarely. I had dined at Vivex more than once and knew important people who would invite me to their houses because they enjoyed my company. I was popular everywhere and had no enemies.

I owned two good suits, but it was my bad luck to meet you in my waiter's apron.

As we sailed farther west there were boats drawn up on the gravel bank, fish-drying frames on the windblown shingle, the doors of a timber shack on the beach half-open, cold darkness within. Slowly we approached land. I could now see turf huts scattered here and there, sheep grazing in a dun field, dark clouds on the hills above. I already regretted having come back.

But you were waiting. You were waiting for me beyond the fog; a distant smile, cold yet warm; eyes that seemed full of kindness—or was it pity? Not contempt but pity. It's worse.

I knew you, but didn't know you. In your presence I never knew which leg to stand on. Yet I couldn't stay away.

You greeted me on the quay, your father hanging back a little. I saw him watching us, a little embarrassed perhaps, and though I took you in my arms, I didn't hold you as tightly as I wanted to.

I had met your father several months before when he came to Copenhagen on business. He had been very pleasant when you introduced us, without a trace of arrogance or suspicion. He had taken an interest in my "studies"—rather too much interest, it seemed to me at first, but then I recovered—and told me about his business trips. He had just come from Spain, where he had started selling fish, and had been impressed by the country and its people. Later on, when I had taken over the company and went there on my first trip, I was surprised he hadn't sold more, as he had formed good contacts. But that's another story . . .

Now he greeted me politely but had less to say for himself than in Copenhagen. He had a cold and kept blowing his nose into a red handkerchief.

I was pretty sure that you were happy to see me. But your thoughts seemed miles away at times, even during those first steps up the jetty, as I was getting used to having land under my feet again. Your hand grew limp in mine, a mist passed across your eyes, and your mouth smiled its half-smile—you were gone. Where, I never knew. Neither then nor later.

I felt as if I were holding hands with a woman in a fairy tale, until you leaned against me and whispered in my ear:

"I'm so happy you're home."

I walked up the jetty with my head held high and the sun at my side.

I didn't know in advance that I would be staying with your uncle and aunt in Reykjavik until the wedding. They lived down by the lake in the center of town and I had the basement to myself. My mother and father slept in the room next to mine when they came south. The house had thin walls.

I don't know who felt more uncomfortable, your relatives being stuck with us or us being stuck with them. On the first day, our hostess probably felt she couldn't avoid inviting us to join them at tea, when their friends came for a visit, but during the following days I suspect she postponed any such gatherings until we had left so she wouldn't have to repeat the offer.

I had bought new outfits for my parents in Copenhagen but neither Mother's black dress with its white collar nor my father's gray suit could prevent them from looking out of place among the family and their visitors in that red, mahogany parlor. I couldn't help noticing their discomfort; father rocked to and fro, as was his habit when nervous, while mother looked alternately down at her hands or at me in the hope of support.

The arrogance of those people. The silent contempt. I could tell your aunt thought she could see right through me; she did nothing to hide her opinion that I wasn't good enough for you. But she said nothing to my face; she didn't need to.

Why did your father arrange for us to stay with them rather

than some other relatives in town? I still wonder what motivated him; he must have had his reasons.

The suit I'd bought my father was a size too big. I hadn't expected him to have shrunk like that. While I puffed at the cigar that your uncle had offered me and listened to my father's awkward attempts at conversation with him and his wife, I suddenly recalled a midwinter afternoon at home when Mother and I were waiting for Father's boat to appear out on the fjord. The dusk swiftly deepened to pitch blackness, a squall of snow battering the windowpanes. But no one came round the spit of land and she held me and comforted me until I fell asleep, exhausted in her arms.

When a work-calloused hand stroked my cheek in the middle of the night, cold and hard from the sea, I half-woke, feeling such profound relief that I wept in my sleep.

And now there he sat, opposite me in that red mahogany parlor. Cigar smoke between us, the lake smooth as a mirror outside the window, no danger anywhere. I looked at his hands and remembered feeling them wet on my cheek, smelled the oars they had gripped and tasted salt on my lips. Thought about the danger he risked. For a bucket of fish? No, for me.

I concentrated on such thoughts to deflect the arrogant contempt which hung over me thicker than the cigar smoke, but it didn't work. I was ashamed of my parents and hated myself for it.

When my father died he was buried in the suit I'd bought him. He outlived my mother by only six months. I looked at him in his coffin and thought about those days before our wedding.

He died in winter.

A few years after we married, when your uncle got into financial difficulties and his wife approached you for help, you asked whether we could assist them, so I summoned him to my office the following day.

I kept him waiting outside my office for over half an hour. The time passed slowly but I tried to enjoy it. When he finally came in I pretended to be ignorant of his affairs, forcing him to spell out how he'd got into his present predicament before he could reveal his errand and ask me for a loan. I said I'd have to think about it and told him to return the following day. Then I lent him a quarter of what he had asked for because that way I knew I'd have him in my power.

He was dependent on my help for years and I always kept him waiting before admitting him to my office. My secretary would bring him a cup of coffee. I myself couldn't work, knowing he was there on the other side of the wall. I might open a book but would put it down after flipping through a few pages, and get up and stand by the window, staring at the harbor, where workers were loading cargo, or out to sea, where a boat was leaving port, or at Mount Esja, white on a cold autumn morning. I would stand motionless, concentrating on the image I kept in mind of my father, sitting in that cluttered parlor with your relatives, old and dejected, so strangely small and dim that I had to concentrate to catch sight of him in my memory.

I tried to convince myself that I was avenging him. But maybe I was just attempting to establish who had the upper hand.

My secretary knocked at the door. She had begun to feel very uncomfortable. "One moment," I called. "I'm just finishing up here . . ."

I don't know whether I ever really managed to convince myself. But one thing is sure: I never felt the anticipated pleasure when I finally opened the door and greeted him.

Kristjan slept badly. The spring night was awake outside his window and he could hear his parents tossing and turning in the room next door. He knew his father wasn't asleep. He had seen Elisabet only twice since he came home; though no one had said in so many words that they were not meant to see each other until the wedding, he knew that this was the intention.

He got out of bed. The pale night sapped all color from the earth, even more thoroughly than the dusk, dulling everything. The blue was drained from the sky and the white church on the far side of the lake was invisible in the bleached pallor. He had to strain his eyes to pick it out. Two more days.

Two more days, and the fetters were already beginning to tighten. The filaments spun from the deceptive freedom of the open countryside and the smiles of people he did not trust. In the mornings he read aloud from the papers to his parents. They sat opposite him in silence, saying nothing when he forgot himself and stopped reading to stare into space, waiting patiently, staring into space with him.

This coming Saturday, at two o'clock, Elisabet Thorstensen and Kristjan Benediktsson are to be married in Reykjavik Cathedral. Elisabet is the only daughter

Walking into the Night

*of Henrik Thorstensen, of Eyrarbakki, and his late wife Margret Thorstensen. Krist-
jan is the son of Benedikt Arnason, fisherman, from Patreksfjordur, and his wife
Helga Eymundardottir. The bride is a pianist; the bridegroom is a graduate of
Copenhagen Commercial College.*

When he was a boy he would sometimes climb the mountain behind the village by himself. The wind would chase him, smoothing the grass before his feet, and birds would glide above his head. As he climbed, the tussocky slope grew stonier with every step until halfway up he came to a patch of green strewn with white and yellow flowers. He knelt, pulled one of them up by the root, and poked it into the front of his sweater. Then he scrambled up onto a large rock under a crag and turned to face the village below and the horizon at the rim of the ocean.

"I'll show you!"

The village shrank beneath his gaze—the jetty a splinter in the sea, the houses like pebbles in his palm—his kingdom, until the mountain called in reply:

"What?"

His voice broke as he shouted from the rock:

"I can fly!"

He knew he could. He knew he had the strength and the determination. He took to the air, above the abyss, the precipice; the birds heeding his command and raising him towards the sky, the rocks echoing his voice, the sun watching from above.

Then all of a sudden he fell.

A sweet smell of alcohol clung to Elisabet's father when he and his daughter came to visit shortly after midday on the Friday before the wedding. He was singing as he approached the house by the lake and suddenly gave his daughter a smacking kiss on the cheek for no apparent reason, twirling her in a circle and shouting as he opened the garden gate:

"Open up, Tomas, and welcome your brother-in-law!"

Elisabet's uncle was startled and Kristjan heard him say to his wife:

"Your brother's here. Were you expecting him?"

Without waiting for anyone to come to the door, her father opened it himself and breezed into the front room.

"Now, how about a coffee at Hotel Iceland? While it's still dry. That was a hell of a downpour this morning."

He refused to take off his coat and sit down in the parlor, saying if he did they'd never set off.

"You and your wife should do a bit of sightseeing while you're in town," he said to Kristjan's father. "It wouldn't make any sense to come all this way from the West Fjords and not visit some of the better establishments. So let's go now, let's get moving!"

He spoke loudly. His brother-in-law tried to avoid going with them, asking whether he and his wife wouldn't be in the way.

"We've just *had* coffee," said his wife.

"Come on," said Elisabet's father. "It's not every day that you're invited out."

He went back out onto the steps, taking off his hat and looking up at the sky, brandishing his walking stick in the air.

"No, damn it," he said as if to himself. "I refuse to believe it'll still be raining tomorrow."

Elisabet went straight out into the garden to pick some daisies. She returned with a bunch just as the others were putting on their coats.

"I'll put them in a vase for you, Gudrun," she said.

"Aren't you coming with us?" asked her aunt.

"No, I'm staying behind with Kristjan."

Her aunt looked at her brother.

"They could do with some time together," he said. "What with the wedding tomorrow . . . There's a lot to think about."

Tomas closed the garden gate carefully behind him, with its number seven woven into the midst of the decorative ironwork, gold-painted and trustworthy. Kristjan had seen the maid polishing it twice since he arrived.

Elisabet waved them goodbye, then closed the door. Kristjan was standing in the shadows in the front room. She handed him the daisies. A sunbeam found its way through the round pane of glass in the front door and fell between them; a butterfly danced in the light.

"Look!" she said.

She took off her coat and laid it over a chair in the front room. Somewhere in the house a clock chimed, but she didn't notice. The silence was overwhelming. Finally she went over and put her arms around him.

He stood rigid, staring in front of him, his hands at his sides. Gradually, however, he moved, dropping the daisies, slowly lifting his hands and laying them on her shoulders. She felt them tremble.

"Come here," she said and led him into the parlor. "Come here . . ."

She walked ahead of him; when they crossed the threshold he took her in his arms and carried her to the sofa where her aunt like to sit. He laid her down gently, then loosened his suspenders.

Above the sofa there were photographs of the family: the aunt beside a round table; her husband posing, pipe in hand; their grown-up children; distant relatives. When he lowered himself on top of her he found he was eye to eye with her aunt.

A smell of cigar smoke hung in the room, the light was gray, a cloud covering the sun. His frantic movements didn't seem to surprise her.

"Let it all out," she whispered to him soothingly. "Oh yes, my love . . ."

A sharp spasm shook his body; he raised himself off her and knelt by the sofa.

"There," she said, "there. You feel better now, don't you?"

He looked down, didn't answer her immediately.

"What about you?"

"Of course, darling. It's enough for me that you're here."

When she stroked his cheek he found that one of her hands was balled. He looked up.

She smiled.

"The butterfly," she said. "It flew to me and settled on my palm. Poor little thing . . . I held it so it wouldn't be hurt. I'll let it go now."

She stood up, taking care not to close her fist, letting the air in through her fingers. He rose too and watched her walk out into the hallway.

When she opened the front door the sun broke free of the clouds. The butterfly fluttered away on its paper-thin wings, was transformed into a spark of light, and vanished. As she turned round, he emerged from the parlor. She went to him, forgetting to shut the front door.

The daisies lay scattered on the floor between them in a splash of sunlight. He watched her tiptoe among them as if she were walking on blazing water.

The rain began just after first light.

He was awakened by the first drops as they vanished into the reddening sea of leaves outside, only a few at first, then a deluge. A squall swept the hillside but the bells remained silent in their towers; he concluded that the wind must be from the north. The leaves swirled in the gust, red and yellow; raindrops streamed down the windowpanes.

He turned his head on the soft pillow and rubbed his eyes. The leaves looked like goldfish swimming in an aquarium.

Summer was over but he didn't miss it. The Chief and Miss Davies, who had been away since the beginning of spring, finally returned yesterday. The construction on the hill had been suspended for months; the summer days succeeded one another in a torpor of heat and drought. The workmen's huts stood empty except for the one where the men responsible for maintenance and repairs lodged. Kristjan and the head gardener had been commended for managing to keep everything going with only half the staff, but neither was flattered by the praise.

It was a Thursday in June when Kristjan had dismissed his staff; the head gardener had thinned out his workforce the day before. It rained on both days, and when Kristjan opened the window the following morning the warmth was gone from the air.

In late June they were paid a visit by representatives of the people now overseeing the Chief's property, to supervise crating up the works of art and antiques and transporting them to the docks. They swaggered around, talking loudly, so that no one could fail to realize that it was they and not the Chief who made the decisions now about what was to be sold and what could remain in the castle. When Kristjan found them in Miss Davies' bedroom, rummaging in her drawers, he had to fight to keep control of his temper.

The Chief rang Kristjan daily to remind him that they mustn't take anything but the things he had agreed to put up at auction, mainly mail-shirts, suits of armor, swords, spears, and shields, which were still in storage in the warehouse down by the harbor, never having made it up the hill. But the list also included ancient Greek vases and several statues, as well as a church ceiling which the Chief had bought at the sale of the Count of Almenas's possessions in the winter of 1927.

For two days in a row an echo could be heard from the tennis court: *puck, puck,* punctuating the silence. On the first day, Kristjan took cold drinks of lemonade and soda out to them on the court, making three journeys with glasses and jugs on a silver tray, as he was accustomed to doing for the Chief. But he didn't like the way they looked at him—"those boys," as he called them when he drank tea with the head gardener that afternoon; he got the sense they were sizing up the glasses, tray, and jugs as if calculating what they had cost and what could be got for them now. He suspected they were wondering whether he himself wasn't superfluous, too.

The following day he stayed in the kitchen when he heard them going out to the courts and let them go thirsty. He had locked the silver tray away in a cupboard because it was one of the Chief's favorites. He thought it was safer.

He relaxed when he watched them drive away shortly before sundown. A golden light still played around the buildings at the top of the hill, but the lower slopes were already in shadow. The car vanished into the darkness. He did not say goodbye to them, but ordered a houseboy to help them with their baggage.

The only point of contention was the silver: the French silver service, which was on the boys' list but not on the one the Chief had sent Kristjan. It may not have been the finest silver in the house, but the Chief always gave orders that it should be used when there were fewer than ten for dinner. And when he and Miss Davies dined alone, they invariably used the French service. Kristjan had objected at first, showing the boys his list and pointing out that there was no mention of a silver service, but when they started asking him about his own arrangements, how long he'd been there, how much he was paid, claiming they hadn't seen his name on the payroll, he fell silent.

Instead of phoning the Chief to let him know, he summoned the assistant waiters and kitchen maids, asking them to polish the silver and wrap it in cloths before it was packed in a crate. He kept a close eye on their work, telling himself that the silver would fetch a better price if they did a good job on it.

When the Chief and Miss Davies arrived yesterday, there had been a brief letup in the rain. Kristjan saw the car stop a little way from the house and the Chief step out into the clear afternoon light. The car continued on its way but the old man stood still for a while, gazing out to sea, then turned and strode up the hill. Instead of coming directly inside, he walked along the terraces and through the gardens, examining the flowers and shrubs, and pausing for a long moment by the fountain outside Casa del Sol, before sitting down on a bench in the colonnade to the west of the main building. Kristjan had to move to another window to see him, as his view was blocked by an apple tree. He watched him for a long time in the green light of the garden. The Chief sat, staring into the distance.

In the evening they ate a clear vegetable bouillon, followed by quails with figs and raspberries, then cheese, pears, and apples. Kristjan had been looking forward to serving them and was cheered by the delicious smell of the birds and the figs that had been roasted to perfect tenderness inside them.

"Why haven't you put out the French silver?" asked the Chief as Kristjan served the soup.

It was as if he missed his footing. He didn't answer immediately, but placed the bowls on the table in front of them, took the napkins out of their rings, and laid them on their laps.

"This is just as pretty, dear," said Miss Davies. "My, but I'm hungry."

Kristjan finally stammered that the French silver had been sent to the auction house. But he omitted to mention that he hadn't dared argue with the boys for fear that it might bring about his own downfall.

"It's not going to the Gimbel auction?" asked the Chief. "I don't believe it. I'll buy it back myself."

"What delicious soup," said Miss Davies.

"I won't let these sons of bitches walk all over me. My silver. You know it wasn't on the list."

"It was on their list."

"We both know, Christian, that it was not on the list I sent you and asked you to follow in every detail. It was not on that list."

"Dear," said Miss Davies, "let's not get excited about some old knives and forks."

The Chief pushed his bowl away.

"I've lost my appetite. You go and get that silver back, Christian. Every single piece of it. You'd better bring it back from that auction."

The rain streamed down the windowpanes. When the wind blew, the goldfish darted to and fro outside the glass. Between the gusts they rested. He closed his eyes again and watched them swim to him beneath the invisible waves.

How was he going to get the silver back?

It was a bright Saturday in December. Snow had begun falling in the morning and continued for much of the day, but now it was cloudless and the stars had begun to kindle. As I walked up the street towards our house, the moon rose over Mount Esja, pure white as if after a long wash.

It was five years since we had moved from Eyrarbakki into our new house in Reykjavik, five and a half to be exact, and I paused to take a look at it before going inside. The date 1911 stood over the front door and I reminded myself that it was I who built this house, with my money. Not yours, and not your father's, but that's another story.

I broke an icicle off the railing as I opened the front door. There was a fire in the living room, I'd smelled woodsmoke out in the street. One of the twins was crying upstairs; I could see Katrin's legs when I came in, she was on her way upstairs to them. There was smoked lamb waiting in the kitchen, and I realized how hungry I was as I took off my hat and hung it on a peg in the closet. I scraped the snow off my shoes, new shoes that I had bought on my last trip to New York. I had been away for four months this time.

I had begun my visits to the States after the war broke out and communications with Europe became increasingly difficult. There were all sorts of problems with acquiring goods to import and no assurance of receiving payment for exports. I felt good in New York, better than in Europe. New Yorkers judged you on your merits, not on your family background.

The twin stopped crying. I could still hear Katrin crooning to him. I couldn't hear you, but sensed your presence. The fire crackled and I went towards the light from the living room. It was yellow and warm, and I stopped when I heard Katrin singing to the child upstairs. I stood there for a long time.

I was wearing a dark suit because I had just come from work. I had recently moved my office; it was now down by the harbor and it took me only a few minutes to walk home, so I would let myself dawdle on the way, taking in the docks and the shipyard, smelling the seaweed and the boats as they came home from the ocean.

The suit suddenly felt too heavy and I was about to go upstairs and change when I heard you speak my name from the living room.

I walked towards the light, flicking some lint off one of my trouser legs.

You were standing by the window in the living room, looking out into the backyard. I walked over to you, laid my arm over your shoulder, and kissed you on the cheek. You gestured with your head towards the window and I saw that you were watching Einar and Maria sledding on the slope furthest from the house. It wasn't a very large bank, but their short legs still had to work hard as they clambered up it with the sled in tow.

You enjoyed watching how solicitous Einar was towards his sister. He had just had his eighth birthday, she was five. He pulled her up the bank with one hand, dragging the sled with the other, held it steady while she got on, then gave her a shove, gently so she wouldn't be scared. He ran down the slope after her and led her back up the same way.

We stood without moving by the window, the yellow light warm behind us, the moon white over the garden. Hand in hand. Suddenly they seemed to sense that they were being watched. They stopped on the way up the bank and looked over their shoulders towards the house, waving when they saw us. Then they came running.

Everything was as it should be. Life was rewarding, gentle, the days full of activity, the quiet nights spent deep in sleep. I stood still and thought about this, and about the children standing outside the window, smiling at us, about the warmth in the living room and the good smell in the house, about you.

And yet—my soul was troubled by restlessness; something was luring me away. My thoughts roamed, and although you couldn't tell from looking at me, and I behaved in no way differently from usual, patting Einar on the head when they came in and kissing little Maria on the cheek, nevertheless I was leaving. Perhaps not the next day, nor the day after that, but I was leaving, all the same. With every day that passed I drew a little further away, with every night, even while we slept. When our embraces were at their most intimate, I was somewhere else. However strictly I tried to get a grip on myself and dissuade myself, sometimes out loud when I was alone in the office late in the day, whatever I did, I was drifting away. You couldn't see it, but I felt I was losing control of myself. And I was afraid, Elisabet, I was afraid of what I would do.

Maria ran into my arms. I swung her round and round the room, her shadow racing across the walls.

"Let's light the Advent candles, even though it's not Sunday yet," I heard you say. Your voice seemed to come from far off.

It began to snow again and when I looked out the window, I noticed that my tracks leading up to the house were disappearing, one after the other.

I always meant to tell you why I sold off most of your father's property hardly more than a year after his death, but I thought better of it. When I look back, I suspect there were two reasons for my silence; first of all, I was fond of your father and didn't want to tell you what a state the business was in when I took over from him, and, secondly, I thought it was natural that you would ask if you wanted to know. But you never asked, not even when I told you that your childhood home would be sold along with the Eyrarbakki store. Admittedly, you put down your embroidery and stopped stitching for a moment, looking up out of the window at the silver-gray wisps of cloud in the deep-blue sky, but then you carried on as if nothing had happened, turning the conversation to other matters.

I was aware of what your relatives were whispering behind my back about these transactions. I have a clear memory of how they looked away when I found them huddling in the living room at little Maria's birthday party. I stopped dead in the doorway, not saying a word, just watching the look in their eyes. Of course, they didn't dare say anything to me, but I suspect at least one of them brought the matter up with you. They will have got no satisfaction for their pains, for they didn't know that you had signed over the property to me the day after the old man's funeral.

We went for a walk along the shore by Eyrarbakki the day of his funeral and again the following morning. The weather was calm during those June days, the sunshine merry on the water's edge. I remember an oystercatcher tripping around us on the first day, dignified and arch, and I pointed him out to you because he followed us as we set off and was there waiting for us when we turned back. When we came out of the church and bore the coffin to the grave, the bird was perched beside the freshly turned earth. It was the same bird, no question about it, dignified and a little cocky, darting away as we carried the coffin past your mother's grave.

You mentioned the bird when we were getting ready for bed that evening.

"Didn't he remind you of my father?" you asked, and I think I nodded.

I clearly remember my feeling of relief when I saw the bird waiting for us by the grave. I don't suppose I had expected him to be there, but it didn't surprise me that he was. I was suddenly overcome in church; I'm sure you remember that I asked to borrow your handkerchief to dab at my forehead, as mine was already soaked. This chill had come over me without warning, this fear of death. I sensed its presence, I felt as if it surrounded the coffin, which stood no more than a few feet away from me with nothing in between. I was angry at first, but when I found that I couldn't conquer my fear, I began to shake. The notes of the organ flew past my ears, the singing brushed my temples on its way up above the coffin and the congregation, above the cross and the water in the font which caught the sunlight from the window.

I was exhausted when I rose with the other pallbearers to lift the coffin, and it was not until we walked down the aisle and the door opened and the blue sky met our eyes that I began to calm down.

The oystercatcher is a bird of the sea and shore, not the heavens. This makes its song different from that of other birds—you can smell the seaweed when it sings. Its share of heaven is like the sea's share of heaven. The oystercatcher is the sea's representative, carrying messages up to heaven. Then it returns, always.

Or so your father once told me. And now he stood there beside the grave, waiting for us.

They muttered, eyes darting, ganging up, plotting against me. Your uncle consulted a lawyer. Imagine! After all I had done for him. But, of course, they had nothing on me.

I want you to know that it was I who laid the basis for our prosperity, because your father was on the verge of bankruptcy when he died. He owed money to banks and businessmen abroad, but at home in Iceland he always took care to pay his debts. He cheated no one and when I took over the business he hid nothing from me, even pointing out where the problems lay. He didn't go into any detail, just slapped me on the back and said: "That's life, my boy, it's not always a breeze."

But your relatives thought I had been handed the family wealth on a plate and hated me for it. They despised the fact that I would sometimes go to sea on my own boats. They thought it proved that I wasn't good enough for your family. They were wrong. I wasn't good enough for you.

I know you noticed how happy I was when I was about to go out on the boats. I remember you encouraging me in your own way. "You haven't gone fishing for a while," you would say. "Maybe it's time . . . ?"

I couldn't give a damn about your relatives. They don't matter to me. But it saddens me if you ever think that I married you for money.

He glimpsed a statue of a white angel in the light between the trees. Its wings drooped in the evening shower.

They heard the first drone of the engine just after four. Kristjan stopped setting the table and hurried to the window, pushing the curtains aside and peering out. The sky was merciless, in the distance lightning struck the bay. He peered out into the blackness, but couldn't see anything but rain and the leaves which the wind raked up and whirled along the terrace. A cluster of oak leaves plastered itself against the windowpane, then twirled away. He looked over his shoulder at the fire which he had just lit in the hearth; it sizzled with a familiar sound and gave off a comforting warmth.

"They can't have flown in this weather," he said to himself as a thunderclap shook the house.

He had expected the guests at three: James Lawrence, the bobsled champion, and his friends Lord Plunket and Lady Bearsted. Originally they had intended to fly from Los Angeles, but Kristjan gathered that they had changed their plans and decided to drive instead. The weather had been uneventful for most of the day, overcast with a light breeze, so it took him by surprise when all at once it grew dark and the window of the pantry blew open with a crash. He jumped, and when he stood up to close it, the rain started. He poked his head out for a second; the raindrops felt warm on his forehead.

He scanned the table once more to make sure everything was right. It was a long time since they had had guests; for months the reception room had housed nothing but silence and memories of happier days. Just over a week ago a kitchen maid had come to see Kristjan and asked whether the Chief had stopped giving parties altogether. Usually he would have tried to make her see that there was plenty in this world that she didn't understand and shouldn't therefore worry about, but this time he patted her on the shoulder and said:

"A lot has changed. We'll just have to do our best."

So it was good news when the Chief announced to him that he was expecting guests. He spoke as if a lot hung on their visit and went over the menu with Kristjan more carefully than usual; turtle soup and duck, fruit, ice cream, and cheese. The duck must be pressed and served blood red in the center. The turtle soup should be just warmed through, not chilled but not too hot. He wanted to see the fruit before it was sliced and served up with whipped cream; it must be soft and ripe, so he suggested straw-berries, plums, nectarines, and apricots. He chose the cheeses himself and wrote their names on a piece of paper which he handed to Kristjan: Roquefort, Gorgonzola, Camembert, and Brie. Batard-Montrachet with the soup, Haut Brion with the duck, old port with the cheese. The sun shone as he passed him the paper, and just as Kristjan was about to leave, the Chief added:

"And have them bring the deer up to the house when we sit down to eat. They'll make a nice view from the windows in the sunset."

———

He went into the reception hall and lit the candles. Rather than retreating from the small glow, the darkness seemed to close in around it. In the distance the clouds reflected a gleam. He opened the front door and the rain slopped at his face, but instead of closing the door, he strained his eyes down the hill hoping to spot headlights on the plain. It was as wild and windy down there as up by the house, the waves crashing onto the rocks. Down the hill the animals were howling; the sound disturbed him, as always, and he turned to go back inside.

Just as the door fell to, the plane emerged from the clouds and flew over the campaniles. The glass rattled in the windows and the screaming of the wind was drowned out for an instant as the plane swooped over the house. Then it was swallowed up again by the blackness.

He ran to give the alert but the Chief, who had been in his study all day, was already downstairs.

"He's going to try to land," he said. "Hurry down and take some men with you."

"Land?" asked Kristjan.

"They should never have set off, but now they must be running out of gas and won't be able to get back."

They drove down the hill in two vehicles, Kristjan and a young workman in front, a truck following behind. The fire engine came later. They crawled down the road and were forced to stop more than once when the car skidded in ruts. Rocks and mud had been loosened from the hillside and slid across the track which lay under water wherever it ran through a dip. They were dressed in black raincoats and boots. It was damp in the car. The windshield was misted. There was a stench of wet wool.

They didn't catch sight of the plane until they were halfway down the hill. It had flown out over the bay but was now approaching the coast again, a speck in the darkness. It approached like a clumsy young bird, at the mercy of the squalls.

All of a sudden it vanished and they fell silent. Kristjan got out of the car, raised a hand to his eyes, took off his hat, but saw only darkness and rain.

Nothing else, until he heard the plane smash into the ground and saw the flames streaming out in the darkness.

When they reached the wreckage, the bodies were still warm. No one was burned, but the redness of the flames played over their faces. The men were badly battered, their limbs in disarray, but there was hardly a mark on the woman. She lay on her back, blood trickling from a scratch on her forehead. Kristjan took a handkerchief from his pocket and wiped it away. Her eyes were closed. She looked as if she were sleeping.

They stretched a tarpaulin over the back of the truck and put the bodies on it, two by two, side by side. Then they got into the car, but just as the driver was about to set off, Kristjan noticed a rug on the backseat and asked him to wait a moment. He grabbed the rug, got out and spread it over the woman. The wind dropped as they drove up the hill; the flames from the wreckage died down. There was no explosion, no smell of fuel.

The Chief was waiting out on the drive. He looked like a ghost. He had forgotten to put on an overcoat and the rain was streaming down his large, white face. He waited while they lifted the bodies down from the back of the truck and looked away once he had identified them, then hurried inside, his movements awkward, unwilling to let his employees see his tears. Miss Davies was nowhere to be seen.

The meat locker was down in the cellar, directly below the kitchen. At the back hung carcasses of lamb and beef, while buffalo and reindeer were nearer the door. It was cold in the locker and Kristjan switched on the ceiling light before they spread out the tarpaulin on the floor and laid the bodies on top of it. He leaned over her, taking one more look. When he straightened up he thought he felt a breath on his forehead.

"Klara," he said to himself. "Why do I sense that you're here?"

He turned out the light behind them. When the others had gone upstairs he fetched a padlock and locked the door.

The doctor was traveling, wouldn't be there until morning.

It was already nine. The Chief and Miss Davies still hadn't emerged from their suite. The food grew cold in the kitchen as the good smells dispersed; the turtle soup and pressed duck, blood red in the center. Cheeses on boards, fruit in a bowl. The cream still waiting to be whipped.

The storm had died down. He blew on the embers in the hearth, warming himself by the fire before removing the unused dishes and glasses from the dining table and clearing them away. All was quiet in the house and the wind made no sound. Walking with slow steps to the window, he pushed aside the curtains and looked out.

In the pale illumination of the lamps out on the terrace, the wings of the angel drooped under the heavy evening shower.

"Kristjan, come here. Quick! Kristjan, come to me . . ."

I started up. My heart was pounding. The sheets were damp with sweat and my thoughts were feverish. They attacked me without warning during the night, in the silence after the storm; fragments of thoughts and half-pictures, a voice which called when I closed my eyes, shadows stirring.

"Kristjan, come here . . ."

"Where?" I heard myself asking. "Where . . . ?"

I got up and went out on the balcony. The wind had died down and it had stopped raining. It was dark. I couldn't tell where the plane had crashed.

A moment ago I thought I was in my office down by the harbor in Reykjavik. I was putting away some papers in my briefcase and had relit a cigar that was smoldering in an ashtray on a table in the corner. The ashtray was made of green amber, in the form of a serpent biting its tail. I bought it in New York on my first trip there. "I wonder where it is now?" I said to myself as I sat up in bed. Then I realized where I was.

In my dream it had begun to rain and when I looked out of the window I saw you dash across the street. You were in a hurry. I wasn't surprised as you always seemed in a rush when you left the house. I put my passport in my briefcase because I was going to New York the following day, for the second time that year, 1917.

You appeared in the doorway. Water was splashing off the brim of your hat, but you didn't seem to notice. You weren't in the habit of visiting me at the office, so I was afraid something was wrong—an accident, maybe. The children, I thought immediately, feeling my heart lurch. I was relieved when all you said was:

"Will you be away as long as last time, dear?"

The light was sharp behind you and your shadow stretched across the floor towards me, stopping at my feet. I could even smell your scent, and when I jerked awake and sat up in bed, I thought my fingers were wet from stroking your cheek.

Had you begun to suspect something?

I went back to bed and tried unsuccessfully to fall asleep. I felt her presence.

When I ran my fingers up her neck, I paused by the hollow at the base of her throat. It was deep, always filled with blue shadow. I dripped some water into it. Sipped it.

"Klara," I said, "the water trembles each time your heart beats."

I heard my name again. In my mind, someone was calling my name.

"Kristjan, come here . . ."

I couldn't lie still any longer and climbed out of bed. The floor was cold, so I wrapped myself in a blanket and slipped my feet into a pair of shoes. The key to the padlock was hanging on a peg down in the pantry; there was a bright lamp burning in the kitchen, so I didn't need to turn on the light in the pantry. The house was silent.

When I had licked up the water, I watched the last few drops evaporate on her hot skin.

There was a low click as the key turned in the lock. When I opened the door I felt the sweat grow cold on my forehead. I wiped it with the blanket before turning on the light. The bulb threw a pale corona on the sheets we had spread over the bodies.

She lay towards the back and I had to step over the men to reach her. The blanket tangled in my feet so I let it fall to the floor. I saw the mold of her face under the sheet. Her mouth seemed to be open. Kneeling at her side, I carefully uncovered her face.

They were so alike. When I said goodbye to Klara there was the same serene expression. I remember how I wondered at this. The grimace of suffering had vanished in a moment, her skin slackened and her mouth closed as if after a long kiss.

I smoothed a lock of hair from her forehead. The cut that I'd dabbed with my handkerchief had stopped bleeding and I had to bend nearer to spot the scratch. Her neck was long, the veins already turning white. Her lips were slightly parted. I smoothed the lock from her forehead once more, before covering her with the sheet again.

Before I left, I kissed her cold forehead.

Summer in New York.

He hurried into the building, pausing in the lobby to adjust to the cool shade. Outside the sun shone white on the trees lining the sidewalk, the clatter of hooves and the rattle of carriages entered with him. The door swung shut with a sudden slam, followed by silence. He removed his hat and took a note from his jacket pocket to remind him which floor the apartment was on. He heard a snatch of laughter outside and turned to see through the glass a young girl running down the street with a bandbox in her hand. A yellow ribbon trailing behind her had snagged on the wrought-iron railing around a sidewalk flowerbed. As she bent to retrieve it he noticed that her neck was pink from exertion.

Andrew B. Jones, Jr., 310 Park Avenue, apartment 10B.

He had noticed the scent of a woman in the lobby and stood still, breathing it in. He guessed that she must have come in just before him, pausing like him to allow her eyes to grow accustomed to the half-darkness, brushing a strand of hair from her cheek and glancing in the elevator mirror before entering. She had no need to remind herself of the apartment number.

He was filled with anticipation but remained standing in the lobby, wanting to savor the sensation while it lasted. His face was ruddy from the voyage and glowing with vitality; when he clenched his fist the knuckles whitened and the veins swelled.

He was free. Outside there was the smell of hope and blue skies, sunshine on a pink neck and people who smiled at you and said: "Welcome back to the Waldorf-Astoria, Mr. Benediktsson. Same room as last time. We'll send up your bags."

The smell of a new world while the old one burned. The Great War had lasted for three years already and there was no sign of an end. Trade with Europe continued to decline, both imports and exports. The Icelandic Home Rule government had signed a treaty with the British that no ship would receive permission to sail from Iceland to Europe unless it went via a British harbor. He could still export saltfish to Spain, but the ships were more intermittent than before and he could no longer rely on being paid for the cargo.

But here there was no war, no trenches, no killing, and ships sailed freely between Iceland and New York. Every now and then some lunatic got the idea of trying to urge American participation in the war, but, of course, that sort of madness found no support. There was spring in the air as early as March. The buds appeared on the trees a month earlier than usual. People's footsteps were light, their faces full of optimism. The days were getting longer, the evenings merry, the short nights passed in dreamless sleep. The streets were washed early in the morning when the smell of bacon wafted from the windows and mingled with the sea-smell from the river. At dawn, birds flew with sparks of light on their carefree wings.

Here nothing burned but one's fetters.

"Will you be away as long as last time, dear?" was all she had said. For the life of him, he couldn't remember how he had responded.

He had taken a hot bath before setting off for the party, ordering a whiskey from room service and sipping it slowly as he soaked in the tub, enjoying the sensation as it burned its way through his mouth and throat. He had left the window open so he could listen to the thrum of the city outside. In the distance someone was playing music. "By the light . . . of the silvery moon," they sang; he recognized the tune and whistled softly so as not to drown out the faint notes that entered on the light wind.

A deep sense of well-being that arrived without warning and needed no analysis. He had dried himself in the warm breeze from the window and dressed in a leisurely way in white shirt and dark blue suit, flicking a duster over his shoes and running a comb through his thick, fair hair. "The silv'ry moon is shining through the trees . . ." The party began at six.

She was wearing a white dress the first time he saw her. "This is my friend, Klara," Andrew B. Jones, his agent, told him and kissed her on the cheek. "Swedish. Dances like an angel. Klara, this is Christian Benediktsson from Iceland. We call him the Icelandic Baron."

He knew at once. As he looked into her eyes. Knew what would happen. He was filled with fear and anticipation, held out his hand to her, releasing hers after the briefest touch. He knew right away, even pictured it in his mind.

They first made love the day before he sailed for Iceland. It was hot in his hotel room, and afterwards they lay in silence side by side, watching the curtains billowing in the breeze.

Now he was back in New York again. The *Gullfoss* had made its sedate progress up the East River just before dawn the previous day. The city was wreathed in white fog as the ship drew near. Here and there the buildings pierced the mist.

And somewhere she was sleeping, under this white blanket. Perhaps Jones lay beside her, her lover, a cheerful young man, practical and eager to please. Maybe she would sense his arrival and toss on the edge of consciousness, smelling the fog outside the window; the fingers of one hand would contract, then relax one by one, her hand resting on the quilt as her lips parted.

The ship sailed beneath the fog. He had arrived.

"Welcome back, Mr. Benediktsson. There's a gentleman waiting for you in the coffee lounge."

Andrew B. Jones, Jr., was an early riser. He got to his feet, putting down the paper he'd been reading, and greeted Kristjan warmly. At breakfast, he gave Kristjan the rundown on business: he had managed to get hold of all the wheat Kristjan had asked for and a little fruit, too, and almost all the sugar, though the iron wouldn't be ready until later. Timber and paper would have to wait until the next consignment. There were plenty of textiles to be had, but it made sense to stock up, as the situation could change.

The Waldorf-Astoria, Fifth Avenue and Thirty-fourth Street. While the city was awakening outside, deals were being done at every breakfast table. No one had time to waste: around the next corner another opportunity was waiting, the promise of a quick profit. There was a bird singing in a cage in the lobby. He was called the money bird.

A waiter wearing white gloves placed a silver spoon on the table, bowed and retreated silently.

Jones stood up. His business was done. They engaged in a long handshake.

"And I don't need to ask whether you avoid doing business with other Icelanders," said Kristjan.

"I only do business with the Baron."

"And I only with you."

"You have my hundred-percent trust."

"Likewise."

They smiled.

"I'm having a party tomorrow at six. At home. I hope you can come."

"It would be a real pleasure. Six o'clock."

"Just close friends."

"Thank you."

Silence.

"Klara and I have just become engaged."

Three-ten Park Avenue, apartment 10B. He glanced in the mirror and adjusted his tie. The woman's scent was stronger in the elevator than down in the lobby. He had two gifts in a bag: a tie pin for his agent, a necklace for her, a white sapphire on a slender chain.

The elevator doors opened. Noise carried out into the corridor. He heard the sound of her voice and walked faster.

When she fastened the chain round her neck, the sapphire gleamed on the swell of her breasts.

Jones spoke with the childish fervor of a man in love.

"The first time I saw her I stood up without realizing. She entered the stage from the left holding a basket, then laid it down on a small table and began to dance. The stage was covered with blue petals and she tiptoed between them without treading on them. They didn't stir, it was as if her feet didn't touch the floor. I thought she was going to float over to me."

He laughed.

"This was no Carnegie Hall, my friend, but I would have stood there for a long, long time if the woman behind hadn't nudged me and told me to sit down.

"When she looked out over the audience, I felt as if she was looking at me."

Jones fell silent, then added:

"Christian, I never knew a man could feel this way."

He seemed unable to stop talking about her. They were standing in a corner of the study, most of the other guests were in the living room. It was evening. Outside electric lights seemed superfluous in the soft spring. Inside were noise and laughter. He was intoxicated, but not drunk. Kristjan listened. There was no way out.

"There's no happiness like waking up beside her in the morning. Rain or shine, I don't notice the weather. I've even started to feel bad when I'm away on business. Imagine, I wake up in the middle of the night in some hotel room and can't get back to sleep, feeling something's missing, tossing and turning till dawn, getting up the moment I see the faintest light through the curtains. Sometimes she talks in her sleep, but I don't understand a word. Is it hard to learn Swedish?"

Kristjan couldn't stand it anymore. He looked at his watch.

"Sorry to run on like this. I can't contain myself."

Kristjan smiled and slapped him on the shoulder. They went into the other room. She came towards them, tall and dark, with a slender waist and long neck, her breasts warm and soft. Her lover held her against him. She looked over his shoulder at Kristjan who was standing behind him. When he finally let her go, she said to his guest in Swedish:

"I've missed you."

Her lover was away on business.

Kristjan was jittery when they entered the hotel together, so he went ahead and waited for her in the room. He knew she didn't like it. She took such a long time to come up that he was afraid she'd left. Just before she appeared in the doorway, he'd convinced himself that he had lost her.

Outside on the street he tried to keep to the shadows. They quickened their pace in the dusk, hand in hand beneath the cold church walls. From the open door came the sound of an organ. Then singing. They paused.

An old woman came out of the church and looked at them. He glanced away.

———

Klara turned around.

"Let's go into the church," she said.

"Why?"

" 'I am the rose of Sharon, and the lily of the valleys . . . for I am sick with love . . .' Isn't that what it says in the Bible? Let's go inside."

The music enveloped them between the cold walls, the candlelight flickering in the draft. Above the altar Christ leaned against a pillar, his hands bound behind his back, the whip raised for the blow. The cross towered against a painted sky, in the distance a glow presaged the dawn.

"Let's get out of here."

"Why? It's so beautiful."

He tore himself away from her and hurried out into the street. The hum calmed him.

The window was open. They had turned off the lights, but it was still bright from the moon. She got out of bed and went to the window, listening to the din from a kitchen somewhere in the courtyard below, reaching out her hand absentmindedly to the moonbeam which fell onto the middle of the floor.

"Close your eyes," she said.

He obeyed.

"Come here. Come to me."

Naked, he rose hesitantly to his feet, took one step forward, then stopped.

"Take my hand. I'll guide you."

When he had taken three steps towards the window, she stopped.

"Here. Right here. And keep your eyes shut."

He stood still. She ran her finger over his abdomen as if tracing a line.

"Can you feel this?"

"What?"

"Above this line the moon's shining on you, but it's dark below. Can't you feel it?"

She stood beside him.

"*I* can feel it," she said after a brief pause. "It feels colder where the moon is shining on me."

He woke up in the night. She was standing in the middle of the room, facing the window.

"Klara," he said.

She didn't answer, just kept moving towards the door. He got out of bed and went to her. She was asleep. He led her back to bed.

In the morning, when he told her, she smiled.

"So I've started sleepwalking again? I always do it when I dream about my sister Lena."

It dawned on him in the midst of their lovemaking. She knelt on a chair before him, her back to him, took him in her hand and showed him the way. He held her hips in both hands. His shadow fell on her shoulders, moving back and forth. He looked up and suddenly realized that in the distance between two tall brown-stones he could see Jones's building. He was shaken and all at once thought he could see him at the window. Looking at him, as if they were standing face-to-face, the walls gone, and with them the panes of glass. He jerked.

"Is something wrong?"

The next day he moved into a room on the other side of the hotel.

"We used to spend the summers with our uncle, the Count. He had a long white beard and pale blue eyes. He collected music boxes and maps. His wife was dead. When it rained we'd read and gaze at the waterlilies on the pond outside. The horses would stand under the great oaks in the rain, but at night I sometimes saw them cantering in the marsh down by the lake. One of them, the white horse that belonged to my sister Lena, seemed to vanish when the moon shone on him.

"We used to sleep late in the mornings. There were flowers in a vase on our dressing table when we woke up, and the maid would open the window and let in the light. 'What time is it?' I'd ask, without opening my eyes. There was a mirror on a little table over by the window; I could see the sky in it when I sat up in bed.

"We drank our morning coffee out on the veranda and read our horoscopes. 'Things may go wrong today but you must persevere. Concentrate on what's important . . .' Lena would be on guard all day, waiting for the unexpected, and I would tease her and say: 'Do you really think you should come out with us in the boat? Something might go wrong.'

"'Klara, stop it,' she'd say. 'You know how superstitious I am.'

"When she drowned I blamed myself, even though it was long afterwards. Her head floated among the lilies as if she had become one of them."

"Kristjan?"

"Yes?"

"Are you listening?"

"I'm listening."

"No, you're not, you're thinking about something else."

"I'm thinking about you."

"You're not bored by these stories?"

"No, I'm not bored by them."

"Because I want you to know something about me."

"Keep talking."

"Do you want me to?"

"Yes, I want to hear."

"We're at a house down by the sea. It's white. The beach is white. The cliffs leading down to the beach are white. Out at sea a boat is slowly sailing. Its sails are white. I have a mouth organ, but my fingers are so numb with cold that I can't hold it. Yet the sun is shining. There's a white tower on the cliffs. All is quiet until I hear my name called. 'Klara, Klara . . . I'm here . . .' I look back and see Lena's face in the top window of the tower. Then I wake up gasping. Always at the same point in the dream. Always when I see her face.

"What do you think it means?"

"I don't know."

"Do you think I dream this because her face was so drained of color when we found her?"

"It's just a dream."

"I know, but I'm so frightened when I wake up. I can never get back to sleep. Sometimes I'm afraid for half the next day . . . Do you know what of?"

"No. What?"

"I'm so afraid that I'll go to her next time she calls."

He had been in the city for two months. Yesterday Jones returned from the West Coast. And Klara disappeared. Her scent lingered in the bedclothes and there was a dent in the pillow, where her head had lain, that he had not smoothed away. The chair where she had dropped her clothes was empty, her voice only an echo. It was a cool day. The forecast for the next couple of days was colder.

He thought of nothing but her. He couldn't help himself, no matter how hard he tried. The *Gullfoss* was leaving after the weekend. His business was completed, the paper loaded on board ship, the timber due there tomorrow. Nothing to hold him. He knew he should leave. The next ship would not depart for six weeks.

He opened and closed his hands repeatedly as he waited for the waiter to bring his drink. Across the street the afternoon sun painted a blue shadow on the red brick buildings. Manhattan Diner, he thought it said over the door, but the white letters had faded in many places, and anyway he had been preoccupied when he walked in off the street. Next door were a tobacconist and barber, further down the street a cobbler, news vendor, and tailor.

He'd never been here before; he'd left the hotel just after three, without knowing where he was headed, first walking down to the East River and watching the boats sailing by and the young people sitting on benches, not waiting for anything, holding hands, whispering to each other and smiling as if sharing secrets. Over the park further down the river, a kite flapped in the wind like a flag on its pole; whoever held its string was hidden among the trees.

He walked along the river, past a fish market where men were busy sluicing down the sidewalk and lining up barrels along the walls, then into the middle of the island and down Lexington Avenue. The sun kindled the tops of the buildings, but down on the street it was cool. The shadow of a bird accompanied him for a while. At Twenty-fifth Street he began to look around for a coffeehouse.

It was good to be alone in this city with its background rumble: hoofbeats, cartwheels, languages he didn't understand. The crowds were a pleasant distraction; he found it hard being alone with his thoughts. He watched the waiter lay knife and fork, napkins and glasses on the table; the waiter wore a white apron and wiped the glasses with a napkin after holding them up to the light. He ordered coffee and whiskey, and drank slowly as dusk climbed the walls of the buildings across the street.

The show began at seven. He should get up, go back to the hotel, confirm his booking to Iceland and prepare for his departure. He knew it would do no one any good for him to see her. Yet he sat while the sun set and the dusk gathered, his gaze fixed on children throwing a ball on the sidewalk across the street.

This morning he had convinced himself that their parting two days ago had been desirable. He even used that word when talking to himself. Desirable. As if he were negotiating terms and conditions, extracting himself from an old debt, writing off a bad loan. He stroked his cheek absentmindedly where she had struck him.

"He's coming back tomorrow," she had said.

They had never talked about him before and he was shocked now that she mentioned him for the first time.

"I know."

"Do you want me to go to him?"

He stood up. Removed her arm from his neck, went over to the window and opened it.

"What else can you do?"

They had been at a cabaret until the early hours with people he didn't know; singing, dancing—celebrating their freedom. It was like when he had been in Copenhagen: free, uncommitted. The sky was beginning to turn gray as they walked towards the hotel; pigeons fluttered between the buildings and lined the eaves. They broke into a run because they couldn't wait to be alone together.

Now the midday sun was shining.

"Let's get dressed and go get something to eat."

"Shouldn't I tell him about us?"

He flinched.

"Of course not."

She was sitting on the edge of the bed. He turned his back to her and stared out of the window.

"I can't do this anymore. I can't pretend nothing's happening. Put my arms round him. Kiss him. Make love to him. Let him . . ."

He turned sharply.

"Stop it."

"I won't . . ."

"Stop it!"

"I can't . . ."

"You've been able up till now."

She lunged at him and struck him in the face. He stood still. She struck him again.

———

Proctor's Theatre was on Twenty-third Street. High Class Continuous Performances, it said on the sign outside. Stay as Long as You Like. Admission 5¢ Balcony, 10¢ Orchestra. Safety and Comfort. Courtesy and Refinement.

He sat in the back, under the balcony, where it was darkest. There was a sour odor in the air. The floor was dirty. The man sitting next to him had food and a bottle. First a young woman played an African harp. She was scantily clad. Next, a man with a wide-brimmed hat made the biggest frog in the world jump along the stage and into a basin of water.

The master of ceremonies retreated as he announced her name. "Klara," he called with a flourish, "Klara, the Swedish Princess, dance to me." The lights dimmed, a red spotlight appeared in the middle of the stage, an old man scattered blue petals and bright-green paper grass under the light, then exited. As they settled on the stage, a thin note sounded in the distance, weak and tentative, then there was silence.

She emerged from the shadows. All was quiet until the note sounded again. Then she began to dance. Kristjan stood up. Her arms opened.

He knew he was trapped.

Somewhere behind the dignified expression in the photograph, the light suit and spotted tie, the gold-rimmed spectacles and brows arched in quiet concentration above them, somewhere behind the speech he was listening to about duties, laws, and veneration for the achievements of the human spirit ("which always prevails, always overcomes evil . . ."), somewhere further down, near the core, far deeper than logic and observation, speculation and deliberation could penetrate, somewhere in the maelstrom of the soul lurked a flaw that could ruin everything.

I put the picture down. It was taken when I accompanied Jon Sivertsen, Iceland's commercial attaché in New York, to a lecture at the University Club in late May of 1918. I remember that we grabbed a quick meal of steak and a beer beforehand and then took our seats towards the back of the hall, near the aisle. It was packed, and I stood up when a young woman came in and couldn't find a seat, but sat down again when her friend waved to her from the front and beckoned her to join her. She thanked me and I nodded. "With our attack on Cantigny, the Germans have now discovered that our offensive is not, as they had hoped, a rabble of amateurs approaching," I remember the speaker saying, though much of the rest failed to register. But it's not obvious from my expression in the picture. It gives nothing away. It doesn't reveal that I was thinking about Klara throughout the lecture and earlier while we were eating steak and drinking beer, discussing business and the boom in the city, the war, and the summer, which had awakened us with a heat wave that morning.

I'm not writing about the man in the picture as if he had nothing to do with me in order to absolve myself from blame. You mustn't think that. I have no one but myself to blame for what took place. But I can't help trying to understand what happened, and though I'm a simple man—I say that without hesitation because we both know it—somehow I have to try to get to the bottom of it.

Don't pity me, Elisabet. Hate me. Please, for my sake—hate me.

The day the *Gullfoss* sailed without me I went alone to church. It was around noon and there was no one there except a man sweeping up and a woman scrubbing the floor. Christ, as before, leaning against a pillar. Klara and I had patched it up the evening I went to watch her dance. Everything was back where it had been before. We had agreed that it would do no one any good to tell her fiancé about us at this point, and anyway I knew he was going to be away on business a great deal over the next few weeks. Of course, it would be more honest to say that I managed to convince her not to say anything. I got down on my knees before her in her dressing room after the show and begged her to forgive me; it was all too easy; I should have understood then how vulnerable she was. It didn't occur to me until long afterwards how hard this game of deceit must have been for her. But by then it was too late. Perhaps I had ignored the signs so as not to spoil our pleasure.

I had made up my mind to go home with the next ship. The *Gullfoss* was due to return to New York from Iceland in six weeks. That seemed like a long time to me and so I never got round to telling Klara. Didn't have the nerve. But that time I stuck to my decision to go home, as you know.

It was early in August. Do you remember when you came to meet me? "Einar's gotten so tall," I said to myself when I saw him on the dock. The twins were unrecognizable—they'd only been three months old when I left. Maria was hiding behind Katrin. You hadn't changed; you behaved towards me as if I'd only been away a few days. Warm yet above me. I don't know how else to put it, Elisabet dear, you were always above me, though you tried not to let me feel it. But that just made it more apparent.

I began to shrink as soon as the ship sailed into port, as soon as I saw the buildings, the roof of my office by the docks, the warehouses, the cathedral tower; shrank until I had become a shadow of myself by the time I went ashore.

Then you took me by surprise. I still don't know what you meant by it—if anything.

"Einar, dear, aren't you going to kiss your father? You remember him, don't you?"

I wasn't sure whether this was intended as a dig at me. You smiled and there was nothing in your manner to suggest that there was anything behind your question. I remember staring at you, trying to work out what was going on. I was none the wiser.

The man with the broom left the nave briefly. When he reappeared he began to polish a candlestick on the altar. His movements were methodical; he had done it before a thousand times. I knew it was childish of me to think that I'd feel better if I sat in a church while the *Gullfoss* set sail for Iceland, but even so I picked up a copy of the Bible, crossed myself, and sat down in the pew nearest the organ. The stained-glass windows trapped the light outside, leaving nothing within but gray shadows.

On the other side of the ocean you were waiting for me. I had sent clothes for the children with the ship. Books and sheet music for you. "I'll come with the next ship," I wrote. "Let Stefan know if you need anything . . ."

It wasn't until I reached the Gospel of John that my hands began to shake. It had always been a favorite of yours and you used to read it before we sat down to dinner on Christmas Eve. I had listened, the children on my right, Katrin between them, the embers glowing in the hearth behind me.

"He that cometh after me, is preferred before me . . ."

I couldn't control the thought which gripped me when I read those words. Andrew B. Jones. Again and again I tried in vain to fend it off. The words echoed in my brain and the picture they evoked left me witless with rage, then utterly powerless a moment later. "He that cometh after me, is preferred before me . . ."

She was with him. In my mind's eye I saw him holding her, her eyes closed, her lips parted with pleasure, the taste of salt on her tongue from his sweat. I began to shake. My palms grew wet and clammy, my hands clenched on the Holy Book. Was this what I had entered God's house to think about? Was this my business here?

I was ashamed of myself, but most of all paralyzed with fear. What kind of man am I? What drives me to this?

Without warning I began to shiver uncontrollably in the pew beneath the windows; beneath the pictures of flocks and stars, a hand caressing a cheek, a cross on a hill. Who am I? What drives me?

The Bible slipped from my hands and landed on the floor with a thud. The old man stopped polishing the candlestick and looked up. No doubt he threw me a look of sympathy, but I felt he was accusing me, as if he could read my thoughts. I looked away.

Outside the sun was shining. I knew she had gone to him. And somehow I had convinced myself that he was enjoying her at that very moment.

The man in the picture is resting his cheek on his hand and looking straight ahead. There is concentration and firmness in his
expression, an awareness that he is being observed, but a certain
nonchalance as well, as if he is used to it. The hair is thick over his
high forehead and the fingers under his hard jaw are long and
strong, his eyes inspire confidence. The girl he stood up for whispered to her friend when she reached her and turned to look in
his direction. He knows they're talking about him but he contin-
ues to look straight ahead, his suit comfortable on his sun-baked
body, light and soft in the summer heat.

The window beside him was open; the damp heat rose from
the street. He watched people moving slowly in the heat, seeking
out shade. He imagined their bodies hot and damp. Someone
outside was whistling a familiar tune and he listened because he
had by now lost track of the lecture. "I would also like to mention
that the economic indicators, in particular . . ." The whistle faded
into the distance, the notes lazy and intermittent, "Skies are
weeping, while the world is sleeping . . ."

His thoughts were drawn back to the previous night; he traced his scar distractedly through his shirt in a quick movement, then rested his hand in his lap.

"When did this happen?"

"When I was a child."

"How?"

"I fell."

"You fell?"

"Or jumped. I don't know."

She ran her finger along the scar. Just as you used to, Elisabet, down my back, under my arm, over onto my chest.

"You jumped?"

"Yes, I suppose I jumped."

"That's no answer, Kristjan. You have to say something more than 'I suppose I jumped.'"

And so I told her what I had never been able to bring myself to tell you. Not because it might reveal something I had hidden from you, but because I thought you wouldn't understand. I didn't dare to tell you about some insignificant childhood escapade for fear of your pity. Not that you ever asked. You stroked the scar with your finger, crossing the border, but never asked.

I didn't fall. I jumped. I stood on the brink of the ledge, above the village and the sea and the hayfields between the houses and the mountain, spread out my arms, and jumped. I meant to fly, I meant to show everybody what I could do. But the birds, which were supposed to lift me, remained high in the sky, and the sun, which was supposed to shine on me, slipped guiltily behind a cloud.

"Poor boy," she said and kissed the scar on my chest. "Did you try to fly away?"

The scar was damp from her kiss.

"Klara," I said, "didn't you ever do something like that?"

Suddenly I was convinced that she was about to tell me something I had begun to suspect, but then she stopped and instead continued to stroke my scar.

I was a child. Yet I'm still ashamed. The scar is a reminder.

The man in the picture has decided to return home. This time nothing will prevent him; he has made up his mind, once and for all. He looks straight ahead and wonders whether there is any chance of his wavering. He has made the decision to end their affair before, especially in the emptiness after sex, only to be overcome a moment later with regret and shame. But he has never actually done it, he's never been able to. Now, however, he is calm; when he woke by her side this morning he found that for the first time he was in command of his feelings. She was sleeping peacefully and he told himself that he would always think fondly of her. He even tried to convince himself that it would be a relief to him to know that Jones would marry her; that she couldn't find a more reliable man.

No one will ever have to know, he told himself, and with those words he felt a surge of simultaneous relief and excitement.

I'm making good progress, better than expected, as I've had more free time than usual recently. The Chief and Miss Davies have been away since the beginning of the month and it's uncertain when they'll be back. The weather has been unexceptional, as usual for August, the days hot and still, the nights cloudless. The hillsides have turned yellow. It's been dry for weeks and the leaves have long since lost their spring freshness. In the gardens around the houses, however, the colors are still vivid and intense, the lawns, watered twice a day, still green.

The wreckage of the plane has been removed. When the doctor came the morning after the crash to sign the death certificates, I took him down to the meat locker. The girl was unchanged, yet I'd dreamed in the night that she had woken up and begun to roam. I jerked awake and almost went downstairs to reassure myself that it had been only a dream, but couldn't summon the courage. I lay wide awake till dawn and stayed away from the cellar until the doctor arrived.

The Chief had a grove of Italian cypresses planted on the site of the crash. It was an odd choice, but I understood when the head gardener pointed out to me that the tradition of planting these

trees in cemeteries stems from what he called their "sacred asso-
ciation" with the Roman god of the underworld, Pluto. It's strange
seeing them standing forlornly down on the plain; I don't suppose the Chief realized that they would draw the eye to the site
rather than obscure it. Miss Davies not only closes her eyes when
driving past the spot, she actually turns her head away. The
chauffeur who brought her up from San Luis the other day made
fun of this when he dropped into the kitchen for a coffee. I
advised him to keep his thoughts to himself.

Yesterday I went horseback riding around the property with
two young men who happened to be staying here at the same
time. One of them was Karl von Wiegand, a reporter who worked
for the Chief in Europe, the other John Mack, assistant to Judge
Shearn, the trustee now in charge of the Chief's entire empire. I
don't dislike Mack. Far from it—he's more polite than many of
the judge's other errand boys, who seem to enjoy waltzing around
the establishment and behaving as if they can do whatever they
please. The words they let slip about the Chief, even in my presence, show that they're too young to understand. But Mack is a
genial fellow, and even though he sometimes makes fun of the
Chief, he's never malicious and never goes too far. I can tell that
he respects him.

Von Wiegand has been here for several days; he's recovering
from a bad bout of influenza, and the Chief suggested that he
should recuperate here on the hill. He sits outside for most of the
day, reading or writing. He looks much better now than when he
arrived, and it's been a source of pleasure to us staff to see his
appetite improving by the day.

Anyhow, Mack asked me to get two horses ready, and I had the
bright idea of suggesting that von Wiegand should join us. They
had eaten together the evening before and—to tell the truth—
drunk more port after the meal than was good for them. When I
said good night they were still sitting, talking; clearly getting
along well. They were looking at photographs from the Chief's

vacations which lay in a porcelain bowl on the table in front of them. The Chief had been going through them the evening before he left; he had sat up very late, deep in thought. Most of the pictures were taken in Europe—Venice, Nuremberg, Bad Nauheim, Switzerland.

"Remarkable," I heard Mack say, before I closed the door behind me. "It's as if he doesn't belong in these pictures at all, as if they weren't taken of him but of a church or fountain or that crumbling wall, as if the old man has been pasted onto the pictures afterwards, the same expression in all of them, no sign of pleasure or indication that he's thinking about anything different than when he left home. No sign that he's on holiday seeing the wonders of the world."

The next morning we set off after breakfast. Mack couldn't keep from making fun of the room he'd slept in.

"The room's octagonal!" I heard him tell von Wiegand. "Between the beams on the ceiling—gold-painted, naturally, just like everything else—there are motifs of flowers and fishes, birds and coats of arms. Do you know why I noticed every tiny detail so clearly? Because I couldn't turn off the bedside light. It was impossible. I would have thought he could afford a lamp that worked."

They laughed.

"The bathroom's gold, too. And there's a huge closet, a carved, gothic replica, like the Riemenschneider altars in southern Bavaria, I'm told, with a bust on top and a Greek vase next to it. The door frames are carved, as well, and the faucets are gold, and the frames around the mirrors are gilded and carved. But there's no tub in the bathroom and hot water comes out of both faucets in the shower. I had to wet a towel and wait for it to cool down so that I could wash. I was going to call downstairs for help, but found there was no phone in the room. And then I discovered just how lonely it is up here. You could yell and no one would hear you. I couldn't even see out of the window for all the gilt ornamentation blocking the view. And on top of all that, there's a notice hanging on the wall: 'Please do not open the window.' It's like living in a prison. Isn't that right, Christian?"

I'd been amused by his description of the room, but I was brought up short by his last comment. A prison.

I didn't answer immediately and it was lucky that at that moment we entered a grove of acacias.

"Do you know why these trees are planted here?" Mack asked me.

"For the giraffes," I replied.

"Giraffes?"

"Yes, we had problems with them at one time. Two of them died and no one knew why. We had to send for a specialist from New York because our vet was at a loss. The specialist found that their stomachs were full of stones. He explained to us that giraffe's mustn't eat from the ground because their necks need to be upright for them to swallow and digest properly. When the Chief heard this he ordered the tallest acacia trees available but they still weren't tall enough. While they were growing, we had troughs built on platforms and filled with leaves so the giraffes could eat in a way that's natural to them."

"Where are they now?" asked von Wiegand.

"Most of the animals have gone, thank God," Mack answered. "Except the bison you can see down there in the valley, and some deer and zebras. The first time I came here, the zoo was full of all kinds of creatures. I felt sorry for them," he added. "They didn't belong here."

I was silent. It had been a good day when they started taking the animals away. I knew the life that awaited them was likely no better than their life here on the hill, but I still was relieved to see them leave their cages.

We rode on. To the east the hill cast its shadow on a long, deep valley. Directly below us was San Simeon village with its post office and diner, its jetties and warehouses, railroad tracks, and the cranes that used to hoist containers full of statues, animals, even whole walls and ceilings, but were now idle. Beyond the village the sea glittered in the bright sun.

"That place used to be busy," said Mack. "But you'd know more about that than me, Christian."

His question depressed me. I cleared my throat and said something to the effect that I hoped the building work would start again before too long.

"Hope for the best," said Mack. "It's all we can do."

They ate lunch out on the tea terrace and drank fruit juice. I had the lamp in Mack's room fixed and called a plumber to get the cold water working in the faucet.

Before he took his leave this morning he took me aside.

"Christian, it's been pointed out to me that there's no record of you anywhere on the old man's payroll. And there are no entries in the books to show you've ever been paid. One might think you didn't exist, my friend. We don't even know what your salary is."

He can't have failed to notice my shock. Without waiting for an answer, he added:

"You haven't been paid since we began to look after the old man's finances. It's been months. You haven't said a word."

"I haven't gone short," I heard myself say.

"Christian, could it be that you don't have a work permit?"

I nodded.

"I guessed. So the old man's been paying you under the table?"

I nodded again. "At my request. It's always been like that."

"How much?"

I named the sum.

"Don't you worry," he said then. "I'll see to this. It's a shame I didn't know before."

"There's no rush," I said.

"But you haven't been paid for months."

I tried to wave his concern away.

"Don't you worry," he repeated. "This is just between us."

Walking into the Night

———

I'm making good progress. This morning I woke up early because I'd made up my mind to try to draw the hawk today. The bird is lying on my table; I shot it yesterday. It had been making a nuisance of itself up near the house for the last few days, stealing food from the outdoor fireplace, so we had to get rid of it. It's strange how its nature is still clearly visible in its eyes, as if death made no difference.

I enjoyed watching the dawn, and before I knew it, my thoughts were as cloudless as the sky and even contained a hint of purpose. There was a creaking sound from the forest and the sprinklers started up in the gardens, the spray soothing the trees and flowers. I took a pencil in my hand, poured a cup of coffee, and sat undisturbed at my desk for more than an hour. The sheets of paper are lying here on the table in front of me, and when I examine the bird now, I'm even more convinced that this was truly a period of grace. I've colored in most of the head, and when I look into the bird's fierce brown eyes, with their black rims, I think I can understand how its mind works. Since I started painting birds again, I have been making steady progress; I believe this is the first time I can boast that I've captured my own thoughts and those of the bird on paper so well that I don't feel the need to change anything.

In August of 1918, I came home for good. It was my sincere intention to stay put. You can see from the bird pictures I painted during the first two months that I had settled down. The shade of chestnut on the godwit's breast and head is witness to the fact, and when I had finished the picture of the snipe, I felt it might start its drumming right there in our living room. I was determined to avoid anything that I knew would depress me; I kept away from the Mozart evenings, for example, inventing business in town or staying late at the office and playing chess with Stefan, who had kept his eye on everything while I was in New York and proved a trusty employee and friend.

Those Mozart evenings—I shudder every time I hear his music. Fortunately that's not often, but I'm surprised the discomfort should have stayed with me all these years.

It was on one of those Mozart evenings that I received the letter. In fact, though it's never occurred to me before, it's a strange coincidence that it should have worked out that way. After a meal at Hotel Iceland, Stefan and I had returned to the office to play chess. I clearly remember that I was playing the Sicilian defense and had the upper hand in the first game. I was delighted, as I usually lost to Stefan, who was a cunning player, so I rose to my feet in triumph, saying I'd treat him to a drop of brandy in celebration of my unexpected victory. I did it to tease him, and he took it in the right spirit, as usual.

When I glanced out the window, over the rooftops on the other side of the street and out over the bay, I saw the *Gullfoss* in the twilight.

"She's coming from New York," said Stefan.

"Yes. Let's go and get some fresh air," I said. "I'd like to hear the news from New York."

That morning everything had been routine, nearly perfect. I had slept well and got up late, past nine. You were up and I could hear you talking to Katrin and Einar down in the kitchen. Katrin was saying: "How well that sweater suits you, Einar dear." And he answered: "Daddy bought it for me in America." Katrin asked you what little Maria should wear today. You hesitated, then replied: "The red dress her father brought back last time." You who were so far removed from such matters—I was amazed that you remembered the dress at all, let alone that I'd bought it on my last trip west. But I definitely heard it. You said those exact words: "The red dress her father brought back last time."

I dressed slowly in the February gloom. In the east a pale gleam kindled a few clouds until one of them began to glow. I stared at it for a while; I felt it was moving away from me but then it drew closer again, cautiously, as if it knew it stood out against the sky. On the windowsill there was a dried flower in a vase; I moved it aside as I opened the window to breathe in the chilly air.

The aroma of coffee rose from downstairs. Katrin was grinding beans. And Einar said: "I'm going to be like Daddy when I'm big." "Me too," said Maria. "No, you can't." "Why not?" "Because you're a girl." "I can too!"

All I wanted. All I wanted was for this moment between darkness and light to last forever, this brief moment that enveloped us and protected us from everything, from ourselves.

The captain handed me the letter as soon as we stepped aboard.

"I was asked to take it the day we sailed," he said. "Here."

I could tell he knew what was going on. He said nothing, but I could see it in his eyes. Had she delivered it herself?

". . . When my father died my uncle took us in. He was called Gustaf. Have I told you this already? I'm beginning to forget what I've told you and what I haven't. Strange . . . just six months since you left. I've always thought Gustaf was a pretty name.

"That year summer arrived sooner than expected. The wind blew it over the lake and I went out into the garden in my nightdress as soon as I awoke and stood there in the warm rain. I was soaked, but didn't feel the cold. 'Come in, child,' my uncle called out from an upstairs window. 'You'll catch pneumonia.' 'Summer's arrived,' I called back. The summer was yellow on the lake.

"We also used to spend Easter at the country house. The lawn was frozen and the snow crunched under our feet. The house was dark when we arrived, with white sheets draped over the furniture. The staff should have lit the fires but they were sometimes late. It was cold while we waited for the fire to get going. I didn't take off my coat. I remember once when I stood in the blue light of the drawing room, waiting for the fire to blaze in the hearth, I glanced out of the window at the moon reflected in the frozen pond. I saw my sister Lena's face. I ran out onto the ice and tried to find her but she was gone.

"I want to christen the child Gustaf if it's a boy and Lena if it's a girl. Do you have any objections?"

I left during the night. I left while you were all asleep; there was a smile on your lips as you navigated your dreams. I left while a round moon shone in the dark sky; when I opened the door to Einar's room I met it outside his window. The light fell on his face, his mouth half-open. One of the twins was sleeping with Maria; I paused by the bed and my shadow fell on the white blanket.

I didn't take much with me; a few photographs, a bird's feather that I used as a bookmark, the fountain pen you gave me on my thirtieth birthday. I took some clothes, as much as would fit into one suitcase, a pebble from my childhood home in the northwest which I carry in my pocket from habit, polished by years of contact with my thumb, and a bird which my father carved out of fish bone when I was a boy.

The day before, I had flung my "graduation certificate" into the trash. You probably wondered where it had gone. I didn't want our children one day trying to find out about my studies in Copenhagen. I couldn't bear the thought.

"Would it ever have crossed their minds?" I ask myself now. Probably not, yet I had begun to worry about it. I even pictured the moment when they found out that my entire education had been a sham. They stood, adults now, by a round table (what crazy things you think up), their backs to me; strange how my imagination made Einar look so much like me. "I don't believe it," I heard them say. "It can't be true."

My suitcase was waiting down in the hall. I'd packed it after you had all gone to bed. I got into bed and stared out into the darkness. You were all asleep. The darkness enfolded us like a blanket and your breathing was slow and regular.

The third step down creaked as usual as I descended the stairs. I moved my weight from one leg to the other to make sure the squeak was the same as ever, then continued downstairs. I remember marveling at how Einar had grown; I could see it so clearly when I stood by his bedside and watched him sleeping. He had kicked off his quilt, and before I tucked it back over him I took a good, long look at him. "He's growing up fast," I remember saying to myself as I went downstairs. "He really is growing up fast."

The case was light; I noticed this as I carried it out into the street. In actual fact, I stopped on the steps outside after discovering that I'd laid down my hat on the hall table and forgotten to put it on before leaving the house. I was about to reach into my pocket for the keys when I realized that I'd forgotten them on the hall table as well. Which is why you found both hat and keys when you awoke, the hat nearer the front door, if I remember right, the keys next to that yellow vase, the one we bought in Copenhagen in a moment of extravagance the day when we first made love.

The ship sailed at dawn for Copenhagen. A Danish cargo vessel that had arrived a few days earlier loaded with timber and coal. The captain was amenable when I went to see him; I got a bunk with the deckhands for a small fee. I couldn't wait for the next ship to New York because it wouldn't arrive for another month and I felt I was hanging in midair, had jumped but still hadn't landed. The sky above, the abyss below. My thoughts at war. The day after we docked in Copenhagen I boarded another ship for New York.

I couldn't say goodbye to you. I couldn't bring myself to. Still less did it occur to me to lie to you about my intentions. I left during the night while you were all asleep. Walked out into the darkness before dawn, stepped into it, vanished.

The sound of my footsteps followed me down the street and for some reason I felt as if they were out of step with me. Then they, too, faded and all of a sudden it was as if I had never existed.

The money. I can't avoid mentioning it.

I'm sure your relatives enjoyed gossiping about my departure, and I can well imagine their remarks on the subject. I could never be bothered to try to correct their slander, but as appearances are misleading in this case, I feel I have to say a few words about it. This time you won't be able to avoid paying attention, though you've always been good at letting worldly matters pass you by.

Before going any further I should explain what state your father's affairs were in when I took over. I've hinted at the fact once or twice in these letters, but never wanted to state it baldly because I know how fond you were of the old man and I didn't like to speak ill of him or his actions in your hearing; didn't want to blacken his memory. So I must insist, in the strongest terms, that you are not to blame him for anything; he was never guilty of any dishonesty, though he squandered his assets and neglected the business, at least in his later years. But to be fair, there were also a number of factors that he had no control over.

The company was in ruins. His business contacts had been allowed to slide; when I got in touch with buyers in England and Spain who'd previously imported fish from him I was told that as he hadn't replied to their correspondence for over a decade, they'd assumed he was dead. It turned out that he owed money to many of those from whom he'd purchased goods for import, and I'd have been better off not to have introduced myself to some of them, as they'd written off his debts. But he had kept up his payments to those he still had dealings with, and they had nothing but good to say of him. That was about half of his trading partners; he seems to have handpicked them as his most important clients.

He'd let a subsidiary company, registered in Sweden, go bankrupt. It wasn't actually registered in his name, but I won't go into that.

I remember often wondering how he'd gotten into this mess; to look at him you'd never have known anything was wrong. To be fair, he did let me know in his own way from the very beginning how things stood, but when I tried to discuss it with him later he would abruptly change the subject. What was behind his habitual mask? Perhaps I never knew him. Yet somehow I suspect that you did. Perhaps none of this will come as a surprise to you.

So that was the state of the business when I got involved in this company that your relatives envied me for. I wasn't remotely prepared. You remember how I worked those first years, you know how I never let up; indeed you often said to me: "Smile, dear. What can be weighing on you so?"

Your and the children's future. That's what was weighing on me. And also—I freely admit—the fear that all those who were critical of me would blame me if things went wrong. To tell the truth, I sometimes suspected that your father had done a thorough job of introducing me to all your relatives the week before the wedding in order to toughen my resolve. "Look," I felt he was saying to me, "what do you think these people will say if you don't manage to save the business? Do you think they'll blame *me* for what happens? Oh no, no one will listen to your excuses. You'll have to bear the blame. You alone. But I'm sure you'll prove yourself, my boy."

He himself had long since given up. But he saw that I was proud enough to risk everything. And I took the bait. Swallowed it whole.

It's not surprising that he resigned himself to your marrying beneath you. The sons of rich families would have run a mile the moment they saw the books, and made sure that everybody knew. And that would have been the end of your father's empire.

We were the only ones who knew, he and I. Apart, maybe, from his friend Halldor, the bank manager, though I think he was never fully informed. Your relatives knew nothing; they thought everything was as good as it could be. But I'm sure they had plenty of theories when they found out what had been in the safe before I left. How that must have pleased them.

I'm not going to get down on my knees and grovel for forgiveness. No, the money I took was mine, and I left behind more than I took, much more. It wasn't more than a quarter of our capital, a third at most. I don't need to justify myself to anyone for not having gone to the States empty-handed. Not to anyone.

I'd better slow down here. Put down my pen, get up, look out the window. I mustn't get worked up, that'll only make things worse.

They must have told you that the money proved I never meant to come back. That's wrong. I didn't know what I intended. I had no plans, was in no state to make any arrangements, it was all I could do to put one foot in front of the other. When I finally came to my senses it was too late. I won't try to justify that. But I had every right to the money.

It was pure coincidence that I had all that cash in the safe the evening that Stefan and I went down to the harbor to meet the ship from New York. It so happened that a few weeks earlier I had received a letter from an attorney in Sweden addressed to your father, who had been in his grave for almost a decade by then. The letter demanded that he pay off his debts to the lawyer's clients, three companies which I assumed had long ago written off these debts from their books. He probably didn't expect an answer, was just writing on the off chance, a debt-collecting lawyer turning over some rocks. Nevertheless, I panicked. I had changed the ownership of the company and done my best to ensure that your father's sins would not catch up with me, yet somehow I was never sure; something had lurked in the back of my mind all those years—the fear that I could lose everything I had worked for.

So I always kept a large sum of cash in the safe, money that no one could touch if anything went wrong. When I got the letter from Sweden I withdrew even more money from the bank and stashed it away. I also sold off some assets, that's true; no doubt your uncle told you about that. But this was the reason, pure and simple. Anything else is the invention of those who you know have always had it in for me.

I hesitated. I admit it. I hesitated before taking the money. But I had no choice. There was more than enough left.

Sometimes I'm woken in the middle of the night by voices from my dreams. Your relatives are talking. Although I can't see you, I know it's you they're talking to. They say: "As if it's not enough that he walked out on you and the children, he stole from you, too. Imagine, from his own children!" And I jump out of bed, unable to control my anger. "No!" I want to scream. "No, it's not true!" When I begin to shake, I collapse, defeated, back on the bed.

Because I know how it must look to you.

The quiet before the storm.

Silent afternoon light in the vines on the slopes, no movement down on the plain. Then the sky darkens and a storm breaks out. The keepers tie a hunk of meat to a large oak to attract the wild animals that have been causing problems on the hill; the clouds race overhead and the air is filled with thunder. I am uneasy. Somewhere out in the blackness I think I hear a wail, perhaps it is nothing but the storm. I stand by the window in Casa del Monte, looking out; a moment ago I sensed Klara was here. It happens increasingly often these days. The memories I thought I could control by writing them down . . .

I didn't know whether she was still living with Jones. There was no mention of him in her letter, no return address. She was fully capable of telling him that he was the father of the baby she was carrying, but somehow I didn't think she had. Why, I have no idea. I also thought about the possibility of her returning to Sweden to be with her family, but that didn't seem right either. I had a hard time picturing her in my mind.

The evening I arrived in New York, I went to the theater and sat at the back, waiting for her to appear. But she didn't and it finally dawned on me that a pregnant woman, seven months gone, would hardly appear on that stage. What a fool I am, I remember saying to myself.

I was gripped by a sudden despair, the suspicion that I had lost her forever. I hadn't had any contact with her fiancé while I was in Iceland, as our dealings had tailed off since the war ended and Europe opened up again. Stefan had taken care of the correspondence with him, put in orders and sorted out payments. I avoided doing so. But now I had no choice but to let him know I was back.

"Are you in town?" he exclaimed. "Where are you staying? At the Waldorf? Always first class. I'll meet you there for breakfast tomorrow morning."

Had his voice changed? Was there an edge to it that hadn't been there before, or were my suspicions nothing but the product of an overactive imagination? He smiled broadly and took my hand in his firm grasp.

"Good to see you. I wasn't expecting you. Hardly get an order from you these days."

A different tone, more careless—no longer the obliging salesman. I fumbled for words, spent too long explaining how much more expensive it was to import goods to Iceland from the States than from Europe, and was about to start quoting figures to support my excuses when he interrupted.

"I'm joking!" he said. "I can't believe you'd take me seriously. Is everything all right?"

I relaxed. Yet I still wasn't sure where we stood. Could it be that she had told him about us? He didn't mention her, not a word. Could she have gone back to Sweden? I asked myself again.

"What brings you here, if I may ask? You turn up out of the blue with no warning. You haven't started doing business with someone else?"

I had prepared an explanation for my arrival, but somehow I found it difficult to put it into words. It had been on short notice, I said. The commercial attaché had asked me to come and attend a series of meetings over the next few weeks, a cooperative agreement with the government in Washington, I said, a gesture of friendship between our two nations . . . I meant to use the opportunity to look around for new business . . . cars . . . electrical goods . . . "You should be able to help me out—naturally it wouldn't cross my mind to go to anyone else."

"Good," he said. "Good. I'd begun to worry."

He smiled and raised his coffee cup as if to drink a toast.

"Business is booming," he said. "I'm sure you can feel it. Everybody is optimistic after the war. Everybody wants to get rich yesterday. And I'm no exception, my friend. Don't pretend to be!"

He burst out laughing. I'd never seen him happier, he must have been making a lot of money. You could always tell with Jones. He was not a complicated man. Just as I was about to ask after his fiancée, the waiter came to our table and told him there was a phone call for him in reception.

"Excuse me a second. Always something."

I discovered I was sweating under my jacket and buttoned it so he wouldn't notice the wet patches on my blue shirt.

"Well, old chap," he said when he returned, "I'm afraid I have to get going. It was good to see you. Let's be in touch. I'm going to Chicago after the weekend, but let's definitely have dinner when I get back."

I stood up to say goodbye.

"It must be getting close to your wedding," I commented as I took his hand.

The answer seemed a long time coming, but that was probably my imagination.

"August," he said eventually. "Saturday August sixteenth. You'll get an invitation."

I was about to ask after Klara's health when I realized he had said nothing about her being pregnant.

"I have to go. Let's meet up when I get back from Chicago."

"When are you off?"

"On Monday."

I waited.

Waited for him to leave.

Wednesday, Thursday, Friday, Saturday, Sunday. Sometimes loitering on the other side of the street, hoping for a glimpse of her, in the lee of a wall, on the opposite corner, but I never saw her, never saw either of them. Empty days, long nights, moonlight crawling on the rooftops like a white cat.

I watched him leave on Monday morning. He was wearing a light-yellow suit and a light-brown hat. I waited for five minutes after he had gone before I entered the building.

There was new wallpaper in the living room, but the furniture had not been touched. The window behind her was half-open. On the mahogany table between the windows stood an opal-gray vase containing some kind of yellow flowers that I didn't recognize. The wallpaper was blue. The sun illuminated it for a moment, then retreated behind a cloud.

I moved one step towards her, then stopped, resting my knuckles on the polished tabletop.

"You're not pregnant."

She smiled.

"Was that why you came?"

"I got your letter. Have you forgotten what you wrote me?"

"I thought you were never coming back."

Silence.

"I had an abortion."

She turned away. I stood still.

"Klara," I said at last. "You wrote me in February. You'd have been six months gone if I'd been the father."

"I'd already got rid of it. I thought you were never coming back . . . I wanted . . . You can't believe how much I wanted . . ."

I was about to leave. I was a second from walking out the door, taking the elevator down to the lobby, running into the street, a free man. But then she reached out her hand and touched me. My fingers first, tentatively, then my arm.

"I thought I'd never see you again," she said.

I jumped. I fell. And the sun shone on the blue wallpaper above us as we made love on the cool floor.

You mustn't think I don't realize how ironic all this is. I'm disgusted by the servile nature that I seem never to shake off, this need to make everyone like me. My heart still misses a beat when he calls me. I hurry to him along the cool passages. "Did he sound as if he was in a bad mood?" I ask myself, quickening my steps, hoping I haven't done anything to annoy him.

But I've always been like this. When I first took over the business, your father said to me: "Kristjan, you're the one in charge. It's as if you forget sometimes that you don't have to ask anyone's permission. You're the boss. Don't go around seeking other people's approval. You'll never get anything done that way."

I never liked being the boss. Not for one minute. I don't know why.

Mr. Hearst can be unreasonable at times. At sunset yesterday evening he went for a stroll around the paths near the house, took a book and sat down under a lantern on a bench with a view of the bay. Miss Davies was resting, she had gone to lie down that afternoon after getting hold of some alcohol. How she managed it is beyond me, but she seems to have become more cunning than ever. The sun was a red globe on the horizon, the trees casting a row of shadows like royal lifeguards at attention on the terrace where he sat; he was silent, lost in thought, didn't say a word to me on the way out. When I peeped cautiously through the window to see what he was up to, I noticed he had put down the book and the magnifying glass and was sitting absolutely still, gazing at the sunset until the lifeguards vanished and the twilight reached the bench where he was sitting.

When he came in again he called me on the internal phone system. I hadn't noticed him return to the house.

"Someone's broken off a rose from the bed in front of Casa del Monte," he said.

"The dogs maybe?"

"You know it wasn't the dogs."

"It'll grow back."

"There are rules. I want you to find out who did it and fire them."

You bully! I said to myself. You can be such a monster when you want to! And all for the sake of a single rose—which will fade away, one of a thousand roses in the gardens around the house. But I said: "I'll do my best."

"Without delay! I want you to find the culprit this evening!"

I knew it must have been somebody who didn't know the Chief's rules. I already had a pretty good idea who it was. For the past few days a new employee at one of his newspapers had been acting as a courier between Los Angeles and San Simeon, a cheerful young man whom I had noticed showing the cooks a photo of his girlfriend.

He had come up earlier that day, bringing papers and films, and was due to head back the following morning. I took him aside. He immediately confessed to having taken the rose earlier in the week, blithely unaware of the dreadful penalty for such a crime. I told him not to mention it to anyone and advised him to drive to Los Angeles that evening instead of waiting until the next day.

"I just wanted to give my girlfriend a rose when I got home," he said, trembling. "Her name's Rose. May I show you a picture of her?"

When he had left, I called together the cook, the housekeeper, and the head gardener and explained what had happened and the Chief's orders. The way they looked at me! Particularly her. The contempt in their faces! Does his dirty work without the guts to object. As if nothing were more natural . . .

Only the head gardener deigned to speak to me.

"That's crazy," he said. "Couldn't you have said something to the old man?"

I was on the verge of losing my temper.

"Why don't you just do that yourself?" I asked. "He's up in his room. Why don't you just go up and give him a piece of your mind?"

Silence.

"He wants an answer by this evening. You'd better get moving."

Of course they found out nothing and no doubt would have concealed the truth even if they had known. But in order to pacify the Chief I didn't dare not to pretend.

"Have you found out who broke off my rose?" he asked as I served them at table that evening.

"No, inquiries are still being made," I answered.

The sat opposite each other at the long table in the huge refectory; I had set the table in the smaller dining room but the Chief was displeased. They seemed so tiny at the vast table, six empty chairs on either side; she quiet, with no appetite, merely toying with the meat on her plate, listlessly pushing bits around with her fork, only a few peas actually making it to her mouth; he hunched in his chair, his eyes mostly lowered. Not a word for the first few minutes. The silver made the only sound in the room. I coughed and he looked up.

"This meat isn't right," he said. "It's supposed to hang for eight weeks, minimum. Eight to twelve weeks. This has been hung for no more than a week or two."

It was approaching midnight when the staff informed me that the disappearance of the rose was still a mystery. The Chief and Miss Davies had taken seats in the theater to watch her new movie. They had watched it the previous day, as well. It had been savaged by the critics; the Chief was apoplectic, Miss Davies resorted to the bottle.

I entered the room quietly. Miss Davies was dozing. The Chief didn't notice me until I was right next to him.

"Excuse me, sir," I said, "I just wanted to let you know that we can't find the culprit."

He frowned and I thought he was about to reprimand me when Miss Davies said without opening her eyes:

"Good."

I seized my chance.

"If there's nothing else, I'll bid you good night."

I felt pretty damn pleased with myself as I climbed up to my room. I'd got the better of him this time; whatever anyone said, I hadn't given way. It wasn't until I sat down at my desk and pushed open the window that it occurred to me what a hollow victory this was.

They came upstairs shortly afterwards. Miss Davies went to bed but he walked into his office. I was wary, but fell asleep in the end.

It was after three when he summoned me. I leaped out of bed, dragged on pants and a shirt and hurried to his room. He lay on a sofa in the gothic library, covered with a blanket.

"Read to me, Christian," he said. "I can't sleep."

"What would you like me to read?"

"*Oliver Twist,* the beginning, just the first few pages. That should do it."

"That's the book that got burned," I said.

"Burned?"

"By the swimming pool last year."

"Something else, then," he said. "Anything."

157

I read the beginning of the *Arabian Nights.* As so often before, I imagined I was reading to a child. A lamp was burning on a table behind me, the other lights were off. When I stood up and went out, he lay still as death on the sofa, his eyes closed, his face long and white, like the marble heads on the statues outside.

I don't know what's come over me lately. I didn't even have to look at the letter I wrote you yesterday to recall what nonsense I'd written; every word was fresh in my memory when I woke up. You'll have to forgive me my ramblings. I should have been more thoughtful when I told you about the finances. A lot more thoughtful.

I wasn't myself yesterday, plagued by a headache and upset stomach, but in spite of that I'm taken aback by the way I sounded off. In fact, I'm frightened by it. I opened the desk drawer as soon as I was dressed, grabbed the envelope containing the letter (it lay on top of the other letters I've written you), tore it up and flung it in the trash.

Now it's calm and sunny and the birds are teasing each other in the hedge outside the window. I feel lighthearted, well slept, and sense it's going to be a good day.

To tell the truth, I have nothing to complain of. I shouldn't go on about the Chief the way I did in that letter. It's bad form. He may not be perfect, no one is, but I'm indebted to him. He's under a great deal of pressure these days, so it's no wonder if his conduct sometimes leaves a lot to be desired. I can't let it rile me. And I should take more care over what I write in my letters to you. After all this time, I shouldn't waste time charting my daily ups and downs.

I'm still amazed, even today, that he ever offered me this job. I'm sure that men much better qualified than I am would have fought for it, but I know he didn't talk to anyone else. We had only known each other a couple of months; when he was a guest at the Waldorf he always asked specially for me to serve him.

Our first meeting came about when I was sent up to his room with tea. This was when I had just started. He was alone. It was ten at night. The moment I knocked, I sensed something was wrong.

I heard him retching as soon as I opened the door. I guessed it was food poisoning. He lay on the bathroom floor in a terrible state, desperately weak. I called for a doctor immediately, helped him into bed (he was heavy even then), washed his face with a wet cloth and dressed him in a clean shirt. It must have taken at least ten minutes for the doctor to arrive. I ran cold water onto a small towel, wrung it out and placed it on his forehead. He was burning hot yet his body shivered and trembled. I had never seen anyone this sick since our little Einar had pneumonia. Do you remember how scared we were then?

After that he always asked for me, and my duties were to attend to him exclusively whenever he was staying at the hotel. Just as well, since he never took a breather. In those days he was happier than he is now and would sometimes say to me before we bade each other good night: "Another day over, Christian, and I haven't thrown up."

I try to do as well as I can and most days I feel just fine up here on the hill. I have nothing to complain of and I'm fit as a fiddle, thank the Lord, and still quick on my feet. Yesterday, admittedly, I wrote something about having been servile all my life, but the truth is that chance alone led to my becoming a waiter at the Waldorf-Astoria. I never meant to stay in the job, and no doubt I'd have turned to something else if Mr. Hearst hadn't spoken to me. But during those years everything was so topsy-turvy that the days turned into weeks and the weeks became months—time was a leaf in the wind.

I well remember the hotel manager's expression of astonishment when I entered his office.

"Mr. Benediktsson," he said, "I'm surprised to see you again."

I won't hide the fact that I'd had a stiff drink at lunchtime to pluck up courage, but I'm certain no one could tell.

"I've come to pay my debt," I said.

It was almost a year since I had left the hotel without settling the bill for my last six weeks there. I had always intended to pay it; you know I've never liked to owe money to anybody.

He raised his eyebrows.

"I'm glad to hear it," he said and offered me a seat. "I always expected you would."

I can't help smiling when I remember his reaction to my proposal.

"Work off your debt? You? In service?"

He was a splendid fellow. Though I was probably the only member of staff he treated as an equal, he was still a good boss to everyone who deserved it. I had just finished paying off my debt in full when Mr. Hearst invited me to move to California, and I can say with some pride that I know the manager regretted losing me.

I only once saw Jones there during my stay; I hurried away before he noticed me. He was having lunch with someone in a blue suit. I didn't see the man's face. Jones did the talking.

"You? In service?"

The manager obviously had a hard time reconciling the man who now stood before him with the Mr. Benediktsson who had been a valued guest at the hotel. As I was about to stand up, he asked:

"Where have you been these last few months, anyway? We tried to track you down . . . ," adding: "We thought maybe something had happened to you."

I hesitated, then told him I'd been staying in Sag Harbor on Long Island, doing this and that.

"This and that?"

I thought it unnecessary to list the casual jobs I had taken during those months that I wanted to forget.

"I worked in a torpedo factory," I said. "Most of the time."

"Well," he said, having decided that this was probably the only way he was likely to get any money out of me. "It's a good thing you've returned to civilization. We'll give it a try."

I opened the door.

"Someone came and asked after you a couple of months ago," he said as I was leaving. "A woman. She didn't give her name."

I didn't pay much attention, simply nodded and told him I'd report for duty the following Monday. Later, when I mulled it over, I realized that it must have been one of Klara's friends from the theater. I had no interest in seeing any of them.

No, I don't know what came over me yesterday. But it's passed now and my thoughts are cloudless, a good smell of coffee wafting up from the kitchen. The gardener is hosing down the terrace, the sun drying the stone. I feel in high spirits.

It's going to be a good day.

Though I don't know how or when you found out, I think it only right that I should tell you when I discovered that you knew I'd lied about my education.

I remember how happy I was that day. It was in the spring of 1915; I hadn't yet begun my visits to the States. I'd worked hard for years to secure contracts to export saltfish to Spain and only that morning I'd received confirmation from my clients in Barcelona that they'd signed the papers and mailed them to me. This was a great relief, as I'd already made investments in order to fulfill my obligations according to the agreement.

God, I was glad! This contract marked a turning point. At last I felt free of the burdens that I had inherited from your father. I told Stefan we should take a break, though it was only just after eleven, and walk down to the harbor, something we both enjoyed, before taking a long lunch at Hotel Iceland. It was no less of a relief to him; he knew about the commitments I had made and, being cautious by nature, thought I'd taken a big gamble.

We'd barely reached the next street corner when I bumped into Svensen from the drugstore. We were on good terms, though we'd never spent much time together; he was a decent fellow, and his elder son had worked on the boats for me in the summers during his school vacations.

"Thanks for your help," Svensen said as we shook hands.

I assumed he was referring to the place on the boat that I had arranged for his son, but fortunately he continued before I could reveal my misunderstanding.

"No doubt your reference had an influence. He's been accepted by the college."

What I discovered after a brief talk with Svensen was that the previous winter he had knocked on our door requesting that I write a letter of reference for his younger son, who had applied for a place at the Commercial College in Copenhagen, as he believed I was a graduate of the school. I was in Spain at the time, due back in a couple of weeks. You promised to relay his request to me, took the directions about where I should send the letter, and assured him that I would gladly provide the reference.

Before we parted he took my hand in a firm grasp and thanked me again. Stefan and I walked down to the harbor. The high spirits that had raised me out of my chair a few minutes earlier had now dissipated, and when we reached the docks all I wanted to do was jump on board one of the ships and sail away.

Could it have been a coincidence that the very day I finally thought I'd saved the company your father had almost bankrupted, I discovered that you knew about the lie which had been intended to make me seem more interesting than I really was? Yet again I had been put in my place. I could work like mad, slave day and night to salvage what your family had ruined, but when it came down to it I was still nothing but a country boy, uneducated, naïve, useful, but not good enough for you. And you wanted to protect me from facing this fact because you knew it would destroy the pretense that our marriage was built on.

Did you think I would never find out? I don't know. Perhaps

you never considered it, perhaps you didn't care, perhaps you thought it was best for me to find out like this. No matter how hard I try, I can't understand what you were thinking.

We were never equals, Elisabet. Not even when we made love. Even then it was as if you were placating a child.

Across the street, washing flapped on a line strung between two fire escapes on the fourth floor, but he didn't notice it as he stared out of the window. The street was coming to life but she was asleep. They had been out late last night. Dancing. They had drunk more than usual. She moved restlessly in her sleep but didn't surface. He watched her for a long time, trying to imagine what she was dreaming.

The war was over. He could already sense the change that was starting to take place in the city. The parties were bigger, the pace faster. And business was booming. Stocks were all the rage. All of a sudden everyone owned stocks, which only seemed to increase in value. At parties people compared how much their portfolios had gone up since last week, since the day before, since this morning. And they didn't have to lift a finger. Up ten percent. Up twenty percent. And the hemlines raced upward, as well, from ankles to knees.

Yet he didn't feel drawn to take part in the boom. He kept a casual eye on the latest novelties that were being invented and advertised, but it didn't occur to him to acquire the agency for these goods and import them to Iceland. It didn't occur to him to join in the game; he didn't even try to ponder the cause of his indifference, but went out carousing every evening with Klara, slept late, made no attempt to do anything practical in the midst of all that frantic wheeling and dealing. Sometimes he vanished for two or three hours after lunch. When she asked him where he'd been, the answer was always the same: to the library to look at the papers. He failed to mention that he spent just as much time reading about birds. All kinds of birds. Especially the more exotic species.

The hotel was cheap but clean, a week cost the same as a night at the Waldorf-Astoria. They'd moved here two weeks ago. She suspected he hadn't paid for the last few weeks at the Waldorf— at least, their hasty departure gave this impression. He had moved their bags one by one, unobtrusively, over several days, and when they walked out of the main entrance for the last time, he joked as usual with the doormen, slipping them tips and asking them to make sure that the weather held fine that day. It was obvious they liked him. He made himself popular everywhere.

His mood hardly ever altered but his eyes could take on a strange look when he'd downed a few drinks. Yesterday evening he'd insisted on introducing her to some Swedes he'd met at a bar, though he knew that she never liked to mix with her countrymen.

"Klara, don't be like that," he said. "They might know your uncle. They say they're from an old Swedish family. From Stockholm, I think they said. They're amusing chaps."

"No," she'd said, "I don't want to meet them. Why are you doing this? You know I don't want to."

"I thought it would amuse you. Your countrymen . . . from an old family like yours. I only suggested it for your sake . . ."

There was a strange expression in his eyes when he said this, as if his thoughts were quite different from his words. She was about to leave when he suddenly put his arms around her.

"Do you hear . . . do you hear what they're playing?" he said. "Come on, let's dance!"

She had never seen him lose his temper. He seemed incapable of quarreling, and she knew he would say things he didn't believe in order to avoid an argument. Which is why she had difficulty believing that he had really been to see Jones just over a week after he had learned of their affair.

"Who told him?" was her initial reaction.

"It doesn't matter," answered Kristjan.

She hadn't seen Jones since it happened; when she had come home that evening her bags were waiting for her down in the entrance hall. She opened her suitcases in Kristjan's room at the Waldorf-Astoria as soon as she arrived. She was taken aback when she saw how carefully her clothes had been packed. There was no question in her mind that he had done it himself. Shirts and blouses folded in one case, dresses next to them, her cosmetics in a bag in the second, along with her shoes; underwear, scarves, and knick-knacks in the third. Everything so neatly packed and nothing missing except the necklace her uncle had given her when was confirmed. The doorman carried her cases out to the taxi. She hurried away; Kristjan sensed how relieved she was no longer having to look her lover—her former lover—in the eye.

Kristjan was restless that night, pacing up and down silently. When she went up to him to put her arms round him, he pushed her away. Gently, but still pushing her away. She broke down. She thought she had lost them both.

"You don't give a damn about me. You're just worried about what he thinks of you. That's the only thing that matters to you. You can't stand it if someone doesn't like you . . ."

Instead of sitting down beside her, he continued pacing and stopped only to say, as he stood by the window: "Don't talk that way, Klara dear, don't talk that way." But she could see that his mind was elsewhere.

It was then that she finally stopped weeping and whispered, rather than spoke:

"I'm two months late."

She didn't believe Kristjan had gone to see him until they received the necklace the following day.

"What did he say?"

"Nothing."

"Nothing? He must have said something. Why do you say he said nothing?"

"He behaved better towards me than I deserved."

"That's no answer. He must have said something."

"He said he'd try to find your necklace."

"My necklace? You must have talked about more than that."

It was hot in the office. Jones was standing by the open window. On the table there were piles of papers and documents. Everything seemed in order. He brushed some dust from the windowsill and blew it off his fingers out the window. He was wearing a light suit and yellow tie, his hair slicked back, his face ruddy from the sun. Kristjan took a chair in front of the desk.

"I'm surprised that you're here. You must know you disgust me. But I'm perfectly calm. Look—"

He held out his hands, backs facing up.

"They're perfectly steady . . . No sign of trembling or shaking. I just wanted you to see that there's nothing wrong with me before I tell you that certain people have been in touch with me. So you wouldn't think this was a momentary rage or some fit that'll pass. Fred O'Connor—you're familiar with the name—and William Green. Or was it Grey? Don't remember, doesn't matter anyway. They said you'd spoken to them. Needed an agent because you were thinking of doing business in Sweden. Sweden! Christian, you must have a screw loose. Didn't it occur to you that they would consult me? Didn't you realize they knew I used to be your agent? I warned them against you. I told them you didn't pay your debts—don't say anything, I know that part isn't true—that you're dishonest and underhanded. Which you most certainly are.

"I want you to hear this from my lips, because I have no intention of going behind your back. I want you to know that I'm going to use every opportunity to make your life miserable."

Kristjan sat motionless in his chair but his eyes followed Jones, who was pacing back and forth before the window. Finally he stopped and tried to smile.

"I can't help it, even though I know you've done me a favor when all's said and done. Imagine if I'd actually married her. I'd be married to a whore. You rescued me, in fact. Yes, maybe I should be grateful to you, Christian Benediktsson—the Icelandic Baron. You're good together."

Kristjan rose to his feet.

"There's a necklace missing that means a lot to her."

"A necklace?"

Kristjan raised his finger automatically to his own chest.

"Oh . . . from her uncle . . . the Count."

"Yes, apparently he gave her this necklace as a confirmation present."

"I bet they were at the country house when he gave it to her?"

"What?"

"I bet her sister Inga had died by then? Gone to float among the lilies?"

"Her name was Lena."

"Really, changed her name, has she?"

Silence.

"Do you still have it? The necklace?"

Jones turned away from the window, walked over to his desk and looked Kristjan up and down for a moment.

"Are you telling me you don't know?"

"Don't know what?"

"Come on. You don't know?"

"I don't know what you're talking about."

"You don't know it's all lies. Make-believe. Her uncle the Count, the country house, the servants, Inga or Lena or whatever she says her name was, the estate owner who courted her—didn't she tell you about him? It's a pack of lies from beginning to end. My God, you had no idea!"

The breeze stirred the papers on the desk before him. He laid a paperweight on top of them, but left the window open.

"It's been a while since I got in touch with a fellow I know at the Swedish Embassy. She's the daughter of a laborer. Her mother died young. The old man died a few years ago. It's all lies. She can keep her dreams as far as I'm concerned—that's what I told myself when I found out. Doesn't cost me anything . . ."

His secretary knocked at the door and poked her head round.

"They're here," she said. "They're waiting."

"Christian's leaving. He's on his way out."

The following day a courier arrived with the necklace. It came in a small box with a ribbon round it. The box was white, as was the ribbon. The package was addressed to Kristjan. "Send my regards to the Count," said the accompanying note.

In the summer I move slowly at midday, when it's hottest. I try to organize my chores so that I'm indoors when the sun is at its highest and stick to the shade if I'm outside. I generally wear a dark suit because the Chief doesn't like to see me in shirtsleeves during the day. Still, my face is tanned and I won't deny that sometimes I long to take off my shirt to let the sun get at my body. But that's not appropriate, unless I pick up a hammer or spade and join the workmen. I sometimes do that, for a change of pace, during the Chief's absences, when I have more time on my hands; I enjoy sweating in the heat from the physical exertion. And the smell of earth and timber and stone never fails to cheer me up.

I feel best during the late afternoons and early evenings. In fact it's strange how much I've begun to look forward to twilight, when the gardener finishes washing down the terrace around the houses. If neither the Chief nor Miss Davies is home, I'll grab the chance to sit on a stool out on my balcony and watch the pavement dry. During the last few days the head gardener has given the task to a young man. I've not seen him before, but he is nimble and thorough. He's so absorbed in his duties that he still hasn't noticed me up here on the balcony. I try not to make a noise, putting my coffee cup carefully down on its saucer, puffing on a cigarette to while away the time in the twilight and watching the smoke curl into the still air like the remnants of a dream. I think about nothing, empty my mind, and never feel better than during these minutes out on the balcony when light and darkness meet and the flowers bow their heads before the coming night.

He keeps his eyes on the ground: short, swarthy, probably from Mexico. Wields the hose with dexterity, keeping up a steady pressure so it's a pleasure to listen to the splashing of water on stone. I must find out who he is, I tell myself, and make a mental note, because I instinctively like this painstaking boy.

The smell of stone rises up to me as the water evaporates from the terrace. The boy has gone and dusk climbs the tree on the other side of the path, before setting off up the mountainside. I can't see the ocean from my balcony but I know it's there. I'm alone. All is calm. And I let my eyelids droop, imagining that the footprints of everyone who has walked on the terrace that day are steaming up to me in the warm evening. I feel as if I can sense what passed through their minds and hearts as they strode past, the girls from the kitchen, the workmen, the delivery boy who brought supplies up the hill in his truck. I can't see their faces but I can hear their voices; they're always cheerful and say nothing that might upset my thoughts.

I amuse myself like this as it grows dark, the water dries on the terrace and the earth prepares for sleep. My thoughts are like a mirror-smooth lake, even when I feel that Klara has walked by. I am used to it and no longer react with shock as I did when I first sensed her presence. Nowadays I always whisper something first—tell her stories from when she was little, as I did when she was dying. She listens; yes, I'm sure she's there, listening. Then she vanishes and I stand up and the night comes to me like an absolution.

I drifted out of control. The days, nights, weeks merged into one; I did my best to waste time, as if I knew that bad luck awaited us, no matter what I did. The money I had brought with me from Iceland was running out, but I didn't care. It never occurred to me that I should make provision for the future; I let the debts pile up and the money run through my hands. Could I have meant for it to end the way it did, I sometimes ask myself. The question horrifies me.

Why am I telling you this, Elisabet? Why don't I write to you about something else, the birds in the trees outside my window, the sea, the sun, something amusing or entertaining that you could even read to the children? I know this is what I should do, but I can't.

It was a long summer. I couldn't make the time pass quickly enough. My body was damp with sweat in the August heat and my thoughts ambushed me when I jerked awake after the partying and drinking. The fan on the ceiling turned ring after ring, whirling its shadow over us as we lay in bed. The clock struck and the pendulum swung but time stood still. I slept through the dawn chorus. She shifted restlessly. The window was open. And a bump, a tiny bump, was beginning to form on her stomach.

I've never been a heavy drinker but that summer not a day passed when I didn't indulge. We woke late, usually in bad shape after the night's debauch, she no less than I. It was difficult to swallow the first mouthful of food, the egg and bacon, which I washed down with a cold beer. She drank coffee. Lit a cigarette. We sat in silence at the café, waiting for our hangovers to subside.

We never spoke of Jones and stopped visiting restaurants and other places where there was any danger of running into him. He kept his promise to destroy my reputation, and I didn't blame him. The people I used to mix with avoided me; now it was mainly girls from the variety show and their lovers who joined us on our journey through the night.

She took a nap in the afternoons, while most days I would go to the library on Forty-second Street to kill time. At five I'd come home and take a bath. Pour myself a glass of whiskey—the first sip was like medicine for the soul. At seven we'd go out to a bar either further down the street or on the corner of Fifth Avenue and Twentieth Street. I'd drink a glass of water to quench my thirst before ordering a dry martini, very cold, with olives on a stick. Then night would fall.

Another morning. Another day.

They returned to the hotel in the middle of the night. She bumped into a table by the door, he grabbed her, kept her from falling. She laughed, sang. He laid his finger on her lips: "Shhh," he whispered. "People are sleeping." She wouldn't let him go, moved to the bed, lay on her back.

"Come here," she said. "Take me."

He took off his jacket and loosened his tie. She laughed, holding his eyes with hers as she dragged her dress up to her hips. He sank down on top of her. When he lifted her dress higher to get at her breasts, the bump came into view. It was as if he noticed it for the first time.

"What's wrong?" she asked.

"Nothing."

"Why have you stopped?"

"I've had too much to drink."

"Tell me what's wrong."

"There's nothing wrong. Nothing."

Yet he couldn't stop staring at the bump, which had touched his belly when he lay on top of her, a little mound like the curve of the new moon in the spring sky.

"You don't want me."

"Don't start that."

"Because I'm pregnant. You stopped as soon as you touched it."

He rose to his feet.

"Don't start this again," he said. "We're both tired. Let's go to sleep."

She pushed him away from her.

"Please, don't be like this," he said.

"I don't want this child," she said.

"Please, not again."

"I know you'll leave us, as well. Like you left your wife and your four children."

He lay awake during the night. He knew she wasn't asleep either. Yet he said nothing and lay with his eyes closed.

For breakfast he had bacon and eggs. She drank coffee. It was hot and muggy outside and had begun to rain. The café was open onto the sidewalk and they sat under the awning; it was green, and the white table top turned green, too, when the sun shone through it. But now it began to rain and a gust tore at the table-cloth and the leaves started to murmur. They were the only ones there; everyone else had finished breakfast and left. At first the awning kept them dry, then the canvas gave way and they were soaked. But they remained where they sat, without moving. She stared at nothing; the coffee was cold and he noticed her absent-mindedly putting her hands over her stomach, trying to press it in. She had begun to do this more often, laying both hands over the swelling and pressing it gently inwards. Turning away from him as she did so.

He felt bad luck settling on them. It was as if he were standing to one side, detached from his body, watching it fly toward them on a gust of wind. He tried to banish it but didn't have the power.

Eventually he reached out for her hand. It was cold and limp. He said something to comfort her. Something about the weather. But it didn't work, nothing worked anymore, it was all over.

The day we went to the doctor it brightened up in the afternoon. It had rained during the morning, but then cleared up and a gentle breeze stroked her cheek when we emerged into the open air. Her hair was pinned in a bun on her neck but a strand loosened and blew into her face. She let go my hand while she paused to fasten it behind her ear, but it loosened again afterwards. She smiled as if to get up courage. I smiled back. She was pale and tired about the eyes; around her neck she had tied a blue scarf that I'd given her for her birthday. The doctor had told her not to eat anything in the morning, which was easy for her as she had no appetite. The white wine she drank before we set off worked fast on her empty stomach, and she said she already felt much better.

She was about four months gone. Two of her friends from the theater had recommended the doctor and accompanied her the first time she visited him. He was expensive but worth it. No quack, he had a diploma from a medical school in Boston on the wall and pictures of himself in a white coat from when he worked at the New York Hospital. He was retired now.

A middle-aged woman received us at the doctor's house. Small and thin, beginning to go gray. She was kind and put a hand under Klara's arm, helping her out of her coat. I paid. Klara still had the scarf around her neck. In the front room there was a picture of a vase of flowers with apples beside it, a Persian rug on the floor. Somewhere in the house a radio was playing, and the low notes carried to us in the quietness. Mozart, I thought, and flinched.

The floorboards creaked as we descended to the basement. They went ahead of me. Klara glanced back twice on her way down the stairs as if to ensure that I hadn't vanished into thin air. It was then that it dawned on me how young she was. It was the first time I had noticed. I was startled. Fear had wiped her face clean of all the masks she had assumed and her eyes stared at me, huge and brown in her white face. I smiled at her but doubted, as I did so, whether the smile would be anything but a grimace.

Could I have persuaded her to change her mind?

"I don't want this child," she had said. "I can't go through with it."

"Are you sure?" I asked. Or perhaps I said: "You mustn't do this on my account." Did I say that? Did I tell her that she should have the child and that we would make a good home for it and cosset it like the apple of our eye? What did I say? What exactly did I say to her?

However hard I try, I can't remember. Yet I feel it matters. As if my words could give me a clue. My words and my tone of voice. What I said and what I left unsaid.

Am I trying to buy peace when I start up in the middle of the night, trying to recall our conversations? Am I looking for an escape route? I'm none the wiser. Yet still I lie awake, listening for the nuances of a voice from long ago, trying to conjure up a picture in the mirror of my mind.

The woman led her into the surgery and gestured to me to take a seat outside. Klara had packed a change of clothes in a bag before we set off and I put it down on the floor beside me. It occurred to me that perhaps they would need the clothes in the surgery, and I stood up and was about to knock on the door when the woman poked out her head and asked for them.

"How long will it take?" I asked.

"Not long."

"Is she . . . ?"

"She's all right. Take a seat."

She went back in. I sat down, then stood up again and began to pace. I noticed that the radio upstairs had been turned off.

During the last few weeks she had asked me the same question every morning on waking. I began to wonder what lay behind it. "Kristjan," she would say, "did I walk in my sleep last night?" And when I answered no, she'd say: "Good, good. Then Lena hasn't been calling me."

Light flooded down the stairs from the floor above and I remember longing to be out in the sunshine again. I could hear nothing from the surgery, all was quiet.

Finally the woman came out.

"She's recovering."

"How did it go?"

"Well. She's recovering."

She fell silent, then added:

"This is the second in a short time. You should think about what you're doing."

"Should I go in to her?"

"She wants you to wait here. She'll be along in a minute."

"And it went well?"

"It went fine."

The doctor must have left by another door. At least, I guessed it was he who had switched on the radio again somewhere upstairs. The tune was lost on the way down, so all I could hear was a faint echo. I was relieved.

I meant to say something comforting to her when she appeared, but couldn't bring myself to. The woman was supporting her. She was unsteady on her feet and her hands shook. I was about to put my arms around her, then hesitated because I was afraid of hurting her. Instead I touched her shoulder lightly and let my hand rest there for a moment, then followed them upstairs.

The street was empty. We got into a taxi and drove to the hotel and did not speak.

The doctor had told her to rest for a few days. When we arrived at the hotel I helped her out of the taxi, carried her up the steps, and put her to bed as soon as we got to our room. It was like going from bright sunshine into a cave. I drew the curtains back and opened the window, then moved to the wall where a shaft of sunlight fell and stroked it with my fingers. Her breathing was labored. She slept. The floor by the window was in daylight but over by the bed it was dim. I was standing on a chessboard, a pawn between squares.

By evening she had developed a fever. She sweated and I wiped her forehead with a damp cloth and undressed her. She had lain down fully dressed, intending to go out once she woke up.

"We'll go for a walk later on," she had said. "To the park. Sit on a bench and watch the world go by. I have a feeling that now everything will be back to how it was."

I undressed her. Her body was damp and hot, yet she shivered. Her belly was still rounded, but the mound was smaller than before. I felt sick when I looked at her.

She was silent. I helped her up into a half-sitting position and fetched water for her to drink. She asked me to pour the water into my palm and let her drink from it. The curtains flapped in the evening breeze and wafted the violet dusk towards us. She finished drinking and stared at the dwindling light for a while. Her face was pale, as if impervious to the blue shadows of evening.

"Stay with me," she said. "I'm frightened."

"I'll stay with you."

"Always?"

"I'll always be with you."

"I'm so frightened. I feel so bad."

"It'll pass. Rest yourself. Think about something beautiful."

She lay back and closed her eyes.

"What shall I think about?"

"Something that makes you happy."

I stroked her brow. She lay still.

"Do you know what I'm thinking about?"

"No."

"I'm thinking about you. I'm thinking about you when you're thinking about me. Isn't that beautiful?"

"Yes, that's beautiful. Go to sleep now. It'll be all right."

I worried that she would sense the fear flowing from my palm when I touched her. I withdrew my hand. She dozed.

When I was sure she had dropped off, I went out. I hadn't eaten since morning and it was now nine o'clock. The night was bright. The moon cast a gleam on the buildings beyond the park at the end of the street, but the light was lost amidst the sea of leaves in the park itself. People moved slowly in the warm dusk, some strolling hand in hand into the park, taking a seat beside some little-used path and putting their heads together. Cigarette smoke curled up in the glow of the street lamps.

Before, when it was too hot to sleep, we would sometimes open the window and lie on the floor on our covers. It felt good making love there in the warm breeze. Afterwards we'd lie still, listening to our slowing heartbeats. Once we woke up to find a pigeon perched on the windowsill. I was startled when I opened my eyes and twitched. But the bird didn't move; a white pigeon with a dark splotch on its head. It looked at me, and when Klara awoke she whispered to me that it was a lucky sign. We lay motionless until the bird flew away. It had been so close that I felt the rush of air from its wings on my chest and stomach when it took off. I continued to feel it long after it had gone. It left a feather on the floor by the window. Klara kept it as a keepsake.

I ate soup and bread at the place on the corner and drank red wine. I wasn't away long, half an hour at most. I brought back some food to the hotel in a bag, in case Klara had recovered her appetite.

She lay on the floor between the bed and the door when I came in. She was weeping.

"Where were you?"

I stooped to help her up. Her body was a dead weight. I carried her to the bed. She wouldn't let me go, her arms clasped round my neck.

"I thought you'd left me."

"How could you think such a thing? I just went out to get something to eat. I brought you some food."

"I thought you'd gone."

"I'll never leave you."

"Never?"

"Never ever."

"You promise?"

"I promise."

I tried to get her to eat something but she couldn't. Her lips were dry and pale and I ran a wet finger across them because she said she didn't want anything to drink. I whispered to her that I was going downstairs to call the doctor.

"Don't leave me."

"I'll be right back."

She was too weak to speak, but her eyes followed me to the door.

He came an hour later. Carrying a black bag, bald, but younger than I had expected.

I stood aside while he examined her. He seemed nervous. She whimpered; he asked me what she was saying but I couldn't hear the words.

"What's wrong?" I asked. "What's happened?"

He beckoned me to go out into the corridor with him. There was no one around. I pulled the door to behind us. The carpet was green, worn through in patches.

"She's got an infection," he said. "She's very sick."

"What can be done?"

He hesitated.

"She'll have to be admitted."

"Where?"

He named a colleague he could turn to for help. He was already thinking about how to save his own skin. I could see it in his eyes, which were small and shifty. I knew this was his main concern and I suddenly lost my temper.

I grabbed him by the collar. He hadn't expected this. Grabbed him and shook him but didn't hit him, although I wanted to. I managed to keep my voice down.

"Now," I said. "Do something now."

"It won't be cheap."

"I'll pay," I said, louder than I'd intended. "I'll pay."

"I'll go down and call," he said.

I let go of him. My hands were shaking. He vanished into the elevator. I hesitated, then went back in and shut the door behind me. I stood still beside it, watching her in bed and listening to my own breathing. It was fast and irregular, but I couldn't control it. The night was getting cooler, so I went to the window and pulled it to. It had been open all evening, yet the air in the room still seemed stuffy. Her clothes lay on a chair. I picked up her dress automatically and folded it before putting it down.

Finally, I sat down beside her. The sweat on her forehead was cold, her eyelids were swollen and heavier than before. I was suddenly overcome with fear that behind them was nothing but darkness. It was then that she opened her eyes. I remember how relieved I was when I saw first the whites, then the pupils. I think I must have smiled involuntarily. Yes, I'm sure I smiled, and I'm glad that's how she saw me the last time she opened her eyes.

"Are you thirsty?" I asked.

She didn't answer, looked around her.

"He went down to make a phone call," I said. "The doctor. You'll be taken to the hospital soon."

"No," she whispered.

I stroked her brow and cheek in turn. It was as if the skin had already begun to loosen from the flesh and I withdrew my hand, then raised it again to push back a lock of hair from her forehead. It was the same lock that had loosened that morning and I suddenly realized how utterly everything had changed in such a short time.

"He'll be here any minute."

She lay still. Perhaps it was my imagination but it seemed to me that she had stopped blinking.

"I'm dying," she said.

"Don't say that."

"We had our good times, Kristjan, didn't we? It was good sometimes?"

"It was always good. And it always will be good. You'll be better in a couple of days."

"It was always good. Even when it was bad. It was beautiful then, too."

"It was always good."

I meant to tell her to rest and close her eyes, but I didn't dare because I was so afraid that the darkness would settle behind her lids.

"Kristjan?"

"Yes?"

"Hold me . . . Lie down beside me and hold me."

I held her as gently as I could.

"Tell me a story about when I was little."

Silence.

"Kristjan?"

I began to talk. I don't remember what I said. At first she corrected me, whispering the odd word, then she stopped. She closed her eyes and I watched the shadow settling in the hollow of her throat. It was like a little dip where the darkness had crept to hide from the evening light. When the breath rattled in her throat and her heart stopped beating, I noticed that the shadow in the hollow quivered.

She stood by the bedroom window, watching the moon glide from behind the clouds above the sleeping town. Somewhere he might be watching it, too, though where she didn't know.

It was three months since he had left; his hat was on the table by the front door when she awoke and his keys lay beside the hat. She opened the door and looked out; the morning was quiet. As the pale sun swept the darkness from the street, a wisp of cloud blushed in the east. His scent was still in the hall, he must have left only minutes ago.

She rearranged the dried flowers in the yellow vase, but left the hat and keys lying on the table. She had protested when he bought the vase because it was expensive but he had refused to listen. She remembered him saying that she would only have to glance at the flowers in this vase for them to open their petals. There was dried lady's mantle in it now and she tweaked one or two stalks gently before opening the front door for a second time to look down the street.

It wasn't until later that day, after Stefan had come to ask where he was, that she had looked in his wardrobe. She was alone upstairs; Einar and Maria were at school, Katrin was with the twins in the kitchen. She had been standing in the same place as now, by the bedroom window, when it occurred to her to open the closet. A shirt had fallen onto the floor and she bent down to pick it up and replace it on its hanger. It looked forlorn hanging there alone and she hastened to close the door again.

Stefan came just after midday to ask where he was.

"He didn't mention anything about leaving. But this letter was lying on my desk when I got to work this morning."

He handed her the envelope. She didn't open it at once but went out onto the doorstep, as if to see what the weather was like. It had rained a short while before, a shower that had disappeared as quickly as it had come, and the street was wet, large droplets still hanging from the naked rowan by the gate.

"You missed it," she said at last.

"Sorry?"

"You missed the downpour."

He nodded.

"There's nothing in it except a report on the company," he said. "It even includes bank-account numbers and balances for business both here and abroad. I don't understand why he's left it behind . . ."

She took the letter from the envelope and ran her eyes over it, before refolding it. Names and addresses, figures, instructions and advice, explanations of various kinds. His handwriting was always a pleasure to behold, elegant and unaffected, in blue ink on a pale sheet. She paused only at the last few lines:

"You're to continue to run the company just as we have been doing. Get in touch with everyone I've done business with, regardless of whether you've dealt with them before. I've arranged for you to have signature authority. Your monthly wages will be raised from today. Report regularly to Elisabet about how business is going and confer with my friend Halldor, the bank manager, about the household expenses and family finances. He will be available to assist you if necessary."

He watched her read, in case he could learn what was going on from her expression. But she didn't look up until she had folded the sheets once more; then she handed him the envelope, smiled and said as she went to the window:

"Thank goodness you missed the downpour, Stefan. Perhaps you should be off before it starts raining again."

She made sure he had disappeared down the street before she locked the door and began to weep.

"He's away on business," she answered, when asked. But by now most people had stopped asking, apart from Einar and Maria, who wanted to know when he was coming home. "Soon," she told them. "If you think about him, he'll be with you."

She seldom left the house. Eyes followed her. In this little town everybody knew everything about everyone. People slowed down when they saw her, put their heads together. With pitying expressions. That was the worst. She had stopped going to concerts. But sometimes friends came round and played with her at home.

The bed was too big. She had considered replacing it or moving to another room but thought better of it. She slept little; retired late and woke early. When she reached out her hand it touched nothing but emptiness. During the day the northern sun was pale and hesitant. The nights were cold. She left the window open at night in case the spring should whisper her a message. But all was quiet, all except her own heartbeat and the creaking of the mattress when she turned over in bed yet again.

Sometimes she got up during the night to watch the children sleeping. She could see him in them, especially in Einar. She caressed his cheek, sometimes speaking to him quietly. He lay still, not even moving when she touched him. She was sure her words were not wasted.

He sprinted home from the jetty, tripped on a stone and went flying onto the gravel, but got right up again, forgetting to dust the dirt off his pants. The sun was at its zenith, the sky blue above the mirror-like sea, a shadow passing slowly over the slopes of Mount Esja. He had been watching it since early that morning but still couldn't work out which cloud was casting the shadow, however often he scanned the sky. He hadn't mentioned this mystery to his companions as he wasn't sure if they'd understand its significance.

He continued at a jog. The boys' insults echoed in his head, though they had fallen silent now and returned to their fishing. He didn't look back until he was halfway up the hill: they had shrunk and the world had grown at the same rate, the road behind him had lengthened and the ocean spread out as far as the eye could see. Yet nowhere could he spy a ship.

The argument had started after they had caught ten flounder.

"Four for me, three each for you," said Einar.

"No, four for me, three each for you," countered one of his companions.

The third boy didn't join in until it became clear that neither of his friends was going to back down. He didn't actually know who had caught four flounder and who three, but backed Einar's opponent because he was bigger and anyway lived next door to him. Einar grabbed four fish from the jetty, shoved them into the bag he'd brought along, and made to march off home with it and his tackle.

"You're not moving an inch with my fish," said the boy, stepping in front of him.

Einar struck him with the bag. The boy hit back. A moment later they were lying grappling in the street. When they stood up the boy was holding the bag.

"Give it to me!"

"You're not getting it."

"I'll tell my dad . . ."

"You haven't got a dad. Your dad's gone away."

Einar backed away. His friends were merciless, crowing in chorus:

"Einar's got no dad, Einar's got no dad . . ."

He took to his heels.

His mother was sitting at the piano when he flung open the front door and dashed into the sitting room. She didn't stand up but turned and looked at him. He came to a halt in the middle of the room, panting, his face wet with sweat.

"Is something wrong, Einar dear?"

"I haven't got a dad. He's left us."

She slapped his face. Not hard, yet nothing had ever hurt him as much. She had never laid hand on him before and he touched his cheek in disbelief and began to sob. She buried her face in her hands and ran out of the room; Katrin came in and comforted the boy.

"You must never say that," she said. "Never say that to your mother again."

———

Walking into the Night

It was good to watch the ships come and go from the jetty. Since his father had vanished he had made his way there every day, after lunch in the winter when he finished school, but now as soon as he woke up in the morning. Sometimes with his friends. Sometimes alone. More often alone these days. Whenever a passenger liner sailed into the bay, he put down his fishing line and went to welcome it. At first he waited, hardly able to contain his excitement, as the passengers disembarked, but no longer. Now he expected nothing.

He gathered up his line, crammed it in his pocket, and headed for home. Halfway up the slope he looked round as was his habit, in case he should glimpse a ship on the horizon, then plodded onwards. The summer passed, leaves fell aimlessly from the trees, whispering nothing to him on their way to the earth.

A new day, but time stood still. The pigeons cooed on the roof, a man walked down the street, shuffling his clogs. Then all was quiet. Things she had heard before, she heard now, but they sounded different. The cathedral bell tolled, a car approached from the harbor, one of only three in the country, climbing wheezily up the hill. Katrin put away the crockery in the cupboard, humming until the silence swallowed the notes.

The anticipated footsteps were never heard and she no longer looked up from her embroidery when someone walked past. Now there was no sign that the comings and goings outside the house disturbed her concentration as she stitched lavender flowers and a church tower onto the cushion cover. Her eyes followed the needle and did not waver when she heard a knock at the door. Katrin let in the visitor.

Her uncle came to a halt in the middle of the room.

"Sit down, Tomas," she said, continuing to sew.

He had grown a little frailer of late, yet the cane he carried was mostly for show. He hung it on the back of a chair before sitting down, dusting some lint from his sleeve. He had always been a fancy dresser.

He asked after the children. She smiled.

"No change since last week."

"And Einar?"

"He's growing."

"Gudrun and I," he began, then hesitated an instant before carrying on. "Gudrun thinks Einar's not very happy."

"Really? And what does she suggest?"

"You know we're all worried about you and the children. You not least, dear."

"No one need worry about me, Tomas. I'm fine."

"It's impossible to help people who won't accept help," he said. "You should face up to facts."

She finally looked up, ceasing her stitching.

"I'm not worried about anyone except the people who are worried about me," she said. "This morning I was awakened by a snow bunting."

He rose to his feet and looked over her shoulder at the flowers and half-completed tower; there were windows running its length, yellow as if reflecting the sun.

"You've never cared about worldly things," he said then, "but I can no longer avoid discussing them with you. It may be that Stefan knows something about accounting, but he can't run a company. Things are going badly. Trade has shifted back to Europe since the war and other people have acquired the agencies. Stefan imported too much at the end of the war without having secured enough buyers for the goods. Both timber and iron. At much too high a price. Now he's stuck with the inventory. The customers have gone elsewhere. It was Kristjan they wanted to deal with. Not some subordinate who suddenly thinks he's the boss. I don't understand . . ."

He fell silent.

"What is it you don't understand, Uncle?"

"I don't understand how Kristjan could have thought for a moment that Stefan would be able to manage the company."

"He'll sort it out when he comes back."

"Dear," he said, "it's been a year. You must face facts."

"How time flies," she said. "And I haven't offered you anything to eat or drink."

"Arrangements will have to be made. You owe money to the bank. You. The company."

"From what I remember, Stefan said the company was doing well."

"When was that?"

"Last year."

When he didn't say anything she added: "My attention tends to wander when people start talking about this sort of thing. I'm sure Kristjan left everything in good order."

Tomas sat down beside her.

"I think it's time I told you a bit more about how he left the business. At first I wasn't sure Stefan had got it right and it took a while to get to the bottom of things. I didn't want to discuss it with you as you've had enough to contend with. But I can't avoid it any longer. You need to know the truth, dear. Kristjan took a large sum of money with him."

She picked up a ball of wool and twisted it between her hands.

"There must be some explanation."

"Well, I don't know what it would be, dear. It was a lot of money. He kept it in the safe in his office. Goodness knows why."

She turned to him.

"How bad is it?"

He seemed unprepared for the question and scratched his cheek before muttering:

"Well, arrangements will have to be made."

"What do you have in mind, Uncle?"

"The company will have to be sold to someone who can run it."

"But when Kristjan comes . . ."

"You can't delay any longer. The company's in both your names. Thank God you have power of attorney."

She ran her finger along the embroidery, stopping at a blue well by the church tower. A stitch had come loose in the middle of the well.

"You've stopped saying he might be dead. Is there a reason for that?"

He hesitated before answering her.

"Someone thinks he saw him on a street in New York. The purser from the *Gullfoss*. He came to see me yesterday. He wasn't sure if he should tell me. He saw a man who wasn't unlike Kristjan. But the man was on the other side of the street with traffic in between. Then he vanished."

"It was kind of you to tell me this, Uncle. Now I can go."

"Go where?"

"There's not much left," she said, looking down at her needlework. "The picture's almost finished. Yet it's as if something's missing," she added pensively, then came to herself and looked up. "I'm thinking of giving this picture to Gudrun before I leave."

He didn't seem to know what to make of her; he shuffled his feet, then repeated under his breath:

"Arrangements will have to be made. I can't see any other way—arrangements will have to be made."

When he had gone she laid aside her embroidery.

She had made arrangements.

Reykjavik faded into the distance as the ship steamed out into the bay: the lake where young people skated in the winter, the milliner next to the cathedral, the two pharmacies, the company she had sold. Barely twenty thousand inhabitants. One missing.

The people who had tried to dissuade her from leaving were standing on the docks, waving to the ship, at least Gudrun was, but her husband had stuck his hands in his pockets to warm them; there was a nip in the air.

She had left the twins behind with Katrin. They were lying on the floor playing with toy soldiers when she said goodbye to them. They hardly looked up from their game and asked no questions, though she hugged them for an unusually long time, kneeling beside them on the floor. She had her coat on; one of them laughed and tried to pull off her hat.

"The poor dears," said Gudrun.

She waited until Katrin had left the room.

"Are you sure you can trust her with the children? You know what she's like."

"And just what is she like, Gudrun?"

"This trip is madness. I can't understand how you could think of it."

The ship was sailing to Bergen, Norway. There they would wait for two days before heading west, over the Atlantic. She inhaled the sea breeze, watching the houses dwindle and the sky draw near. Maria hummed. Einar was silent.

"There's our house," Maria said suddenly. "Look, Einar, there it is."

A white house with a red roof watched them from the hill, the curtains pulled back, eyes on the other side of the windowpanes which reflected the sky. Then it was as if the house were freed from the earth and merged into the veil of cloud above the town, floating up into the air, vanishing.

The shrill cries of seabirds pursued them. Einar saw the jetty where he was accustomed to sit and gaze out to sea; the shed wall above, in whose shelter one could stand and dream. Then the jetty and the shed were lost in the vastness, while the sea rose and fell, the waves rushing like carefree children up the rocks before plunging back down into the sea.

"I didn't mean you should sell everything immediately," her uncle had said. "Think what you're doing. There's no need to rush into anything. It was only yesterday that I mentioned this to you. I wanted to warn you so you'd know where you stand. This sort of thing takes time. You'll make a worse mess if you charge ahead like this."

She wouldn't be deflected. She was going on a trip. She had checked the sailing times and made arrangements to buy a passage for herself and the two older children. When her uncle tried to talk her out of it, she said she had been in touch with the bank manager and asked him to sell the company.

"I should never have mentioned what that purser said. He thought he'd caught a glimpse of a man. In the distance. And now you're planning to sell everything you own and go off after a will-o'-the-wisp with the children. You're not right in the head, dear."

She handed him the embroidery.

"I've finally finished this. Please, would you do me a favor and give this little gift to Gudrun?"

"Elisabet, let me help you. I can't just stand by and watch you charge off into the unknown."

"The unknown is here. I don't need to go anywhere to find it. But I know he's waiting for me. I know he needs me."

"I don't want to say anything to hurt you but in the unlikely event that it was Kristjan in New York, why do you think he hasn't got in touch?"

She smiled faintly.

"I know him. He's lost his way. I need to help him back."

They took rooms at a pensione down by the harbor in Bergen. It was raining and the fjord was hidden by fog. On the second day she was told that the ship which was to have taken them to New York had developed engine trouble. The next crossing would not be for three weeks.

She cut out pictures from the newspapers of people sitting and walking, of boats afloat on rivers, of palaces, horses and bridges, arranging them on the table in their room and making up stories about the people who lived in the palaces, about the boats which sailed up the rivers in front of the palaces and the man who stood on the bridge and watched the boats. "He's called Napoleon Bonaparte," she said. "He's going to save the world."

The sea breeze buffeted the house; they heard the neighing cry of a capercaillie when she opened the window. She kept her money in a bag which she never let out of her sight unless Einar was there to keep an eye on it. When she went for a walk with Maria, he stayed behind in their room. As soon as they came back, he went out.

He walked the same way every day, along the shore and up a hill where an old mill was beginning to break free from the wintry ice. The redpoll had arrived and the dunlin, too; he recognized them at once and cheered up when he spotted them. It was like meeting old friends.

The hillside was wet and black with the thaw; his shoes squished as he walked toward the mill. Beyond was the sea. Boats casting their anchors. The way to his father lay over the waves.

The days passed slowly. The delay was making a hole in their funds; she hadn't envisaged having to pay their keep for three weeks in Bergen. Einar knew this and tried to hold back at mealtimes. She noticed and bought more than he could eat. It kept on raining. The mill was silent, streams trickled down the hillside with a quiet purling.

The way out lay like a path through the waves of the fjord. He had seen it. The wake of a dream. When he woke up one morning, the ship had docked.

They sailed up the Hudson at daybreak. Land had been sighted an hour before; all the passengers had come up on deck to watch the dawn float towards them down the river, the buildings rising from the waves and hope coming to them on the hot wind. They were quiet, solemn, whispering if they needed to speak.

Maria tugged at the hem of her mother's skirt.

"Is Daddy there? Will he be there to meet us?"

The first mate called out the passengers' names for the last time before they disembarked. He stood by the gangway with the passenger list, calling them one at a time. Elisabet was number 29, Einar 30, Maria 31. They had pinned labels to their coats with their numbers and the name of the ship, *Bergensfjord*. Printed at the top of the label was: "Landing Card."

A ferry carried them downriver to Ellis Island. The sun was hot on the wooden roof, the windows were locked. There were four ferries ahead of them so they would have to wait until midday. It grew hotter, babies cried, the air was heavy and humid. "Yes, thank you very much," an old man muttered to himself over and over again, "thank you very much. I'm from Norway. Healthy. Very healthy, sir."

People wore their Sunday best, some of the women had lace dresses, boys wore sailor suits, men wore shirts buttoned up to the neck. One or two men sported ties; most wore hats or peaked caps. Some of the clothes were threadbare but clean. The women were all wearing hats.

They had no sooner disembarked than they were swallowed up by an imposing, brick building. "Baggage Room," announced a guard, but she didn't dare to be parted from the case containing her money and papers, so she continued up the stairs. Maria was tired and whimpered. She pulled her along behind her.

"It's all right, we're almost there."

The child dragged her feet.

"I'm so thirsty."

A doctor stood at the top of the stairs, watching the passengers as they climbed up.

"Is she ill?" he asked.

"Sorry?" said Elisabet.

"Ill?"

"No."

She handed him their health certificates. He seemed to take a long time reading them. He looked back at Maria. Finally he stamped the papers and motioned to them to continue.

Next they entered the Registration Room, where another doctor received them. The old man who had been constantly practicing "thank you very much" and "very healthy" while they waited on the ferry was in the line ahead of them. But now it was as if he had lost his tongue; he cleared his throat several times but stopped when the doctor removed his hat and began to examine his scalp. It wasn't until the doctor wrote "sc" in chalk on his coat collar that the man stammered that he was very healthy. But it made no difference, he had been marked. He was taken out of the line and sent for further examination.

The doctor was quick to examine Elisabet and the children, and so were the next two doctors who succeeded him. They sat down on a bench in the middle of the Registration Room and waited for their numbers to be called. The immigration officials were at the back of the room, dressed in black uniforms and caps. Their desks reminded Elisabet of the counter in her father's store in Eyrarbakki. She smiled at the thought: it was a good omen.

"Twenty-nine!"

They hurried across the room. Einar held Maria's hand.

"What's your name? And the children? What are their names?"

There was an interpreter beside the immigration official; she was relieved because she was unaccustomed to speaking English. Though she managed by herself at first.

"How much money do you have with you?"

She answered.

"Married or single?"

"Married."

"Purpose of your visit."

"My husband . . ."

She glanced at the interpreter. The official nodded to indicate that she could speak Danish.

"I've come to see my husband."

"Where is he?"

"He's here in America."

"Where in America?"

"Here in New York, I think."

"You think? You're not sure? Isn't he coming to meet you?"

"I've come to look for him."

The official turned to the interpreter. They spoke together in English.

"Do you have anyone else here?" the interpreter asked finally.

"We have relatives in Dakota."

"Have they come to meet you?"

"No."

"So you're traveling alone? With the children. To look for your husband?"

Silence.

The immigration official continued to speak to the interpreter, who listened, nodded, then turned to her.

"You'll have to stay here. It's not permitted for a woman with children to enter the country if there's no one to be responsible for them. You have enough money to pay for board and lodging for a few weeks, but there's no telling what'll happen after that. You'll have to stay here until your husband comes to meet you . . ."

"My husband is lost."

"I'm sorry? Lost?" he exclaimed but decided not to ask any more.

"If your relatives in Dakota send a telegram and undertake to be responsible for your welfare, you will be allowed to go to them by train from here."

"Not to New York?"

"Not unless you have someone in New York."

She had been holding the bag, but now she put it down.

"What's the matter, Mamma?" asked Einar.

"Nothing, dear. We'll be staying here for a few days."

"Thirty-eight!" she heard the immigration official call out as they were led away.

At night the city lights were visible across the harbor. She lay awake; Maria was asleep in the bunk below her, Einar above. In the bunk at her feet slept a Turkish woman. If she glanced up she looked straight at the shoes of a woman from Hungary. They were worn through.

They slept on canvas stretched over an iron frame; they were allotted two blankets each, one to sleep on, another to cover them. The blankets Maria was given turned out to be infested with lice. Elisabet gave her one of her own. They could sleep on the bare canvas. There were three hundred women and children in the dormitory.

She listened to the city as she lay awake. It was not so much noise as breathing, giving the hint of a rapid heartbeat. She had her bag in her bunk with her; yesterday she dreamed that the Turk was trying to steal it while she slept.

They were allowed out in the open air for two hours a day. She encouraged Einar to take exercise, run about, hop and jump, because he seemed apathetic and showed a tendency to stand aloof, gazing across the harbor. Maria whined; she told her stories to keep her amused. She missed having newspapers from which to cut photos and drawings.

Most people behaved as if they were under surveillance and believed that even their gait and bearing could influence whether they were allowed into the country or not. A respectably dressed couple promenaded sedately around the compound, their arms linked, the husband leading their young son by the hand. Their deportment was not achieved without effort. All at once the boy began to drag his feet. His father's expression did not alter but his grip tightened on the child's hand. They carried on walking. The woman held her head high, staring into midair. The boy's movements became more awkward with every step, but his father looked straight ahead, his knuckles white. When the child managed to stop for a moment, a turd slid out of his trouser leg. His father swooped and snatched it up in a handkerchief, quickly pocketing it.

Elisabet's eyes met them. They shot her a look that implored her not to tell anyone.

The days passed. At night the electric lights outside were reflected in the dormitory. She was calm because she had made arrangements. A relation of hers, Hans Thorstensen, a pastor and farmer in North Dakota, was on his way by train to the city to meet them. They were first cousins but had never met. Her father's brother had emigrated to America when he was young and subsequently had four children. Hans was the eldest. He was going to take Einar and Maria home with him while she searched for Kristjan in New York. He had undertaken in writing to be responsible for supporting them, but it was Elisabet who paid for the train tickets. They didn't mention this arrangement to the immigration office.

Most meals were basic—stewed prunes, porridge—but there

was meat stew on Wednesdays, with bread and sometimes bananas. They didn't go hungry. The dining room sat twelve hundred people. On Sundays there was ice cream for dessert. On Mondays there was corn on the cob. In the evening the children were given warm milk and cookies. At night three hundred dreams roamed in their dormitory.

They had been on Ellis Island for two weeks when Hans Thorstensen came to fetch them. He tried to pass as a local, though in fact he had never been to the big city before. He wore a dark suit and a hat, and in his right hand he carried a leather case with the monogram jTh. It had been his father's. He reached inside the case for a fountain pen to sign the papers he was handed. He read them first, then put on his glasses and frowned as he removed the top from the pen, nodding to himself as if to show that he agreed to what he was signing and would therefore make no objections. His manner was dignified during this procedure, even commanding, though he knew that in this place he had no choice. Then he hugged his cousin and patted the children on the head. Einar thought he looked like the photograph of his grandfather in the living room at home in Reykjavik.

It's strange how some people carry an aura of security with them wherever they go; it's as if it travels a few paces ahead of them and announces their arrival. The children sensed it the moment their cousin approached them across the waiting room. Their hearts lifted. Maria slipped her hand into his.

Before they left the island, Hans changed Elisabet's Danish kroner into dollars and bought her a ticket for the ferry to the Battery on the southern tip of Manhattan. However, he changed only a fraction of her money, as he knew the rates would be better in the banks in the city. He had reserved a room for her at a cheap but clean guesthouse and written directions for her in a notebook which he put in her hand. Translations of words and phrases, the price of necessities, a description of the big city which he had found at the library in Grand Forks.

The breeze was blowing from the south when she boarded the ferry. In a few minutes the children would take another ferry with their cousin to the railroad station in Jersey City. He was going to take them to a place where the yellow fields rippled like a calm sea at sunset.

They saw the wind stirring her hair, then she vanished as the boat headed for the city.

As his cousin led them up the quay, Einar was ashamed at how easy he had found it to say goodbye to his mother.

The Waldorf-Astoria.

She knew he used to stay here. She could sense that he had been there as soon as she walked into the lobby and looked down the long, blue carpet which flowed along the wide hall like a river. The marble walls gave off a chill; it was hot outside and she stopped to get her breath, wiping pearls of sweat from her brow. She looked down: he had walked here, perhaps she was treading in his footsteps.

The man in reception didn't understand at first when she said his name, then finally realized that the name obscured by her pronunciation was familiar to him. He asked her to wait, went out through a door behind, then returned with his superior, a man of around forty, she guessed, short with a mustache and wet-combed hair.

"Assistant Manager" was printed on the card he handed her.

She repeated the name. "Kristjan Benediktsson. Is he staying here?"

The man smiled. He explained that Mr. Benediktsson had stayed here more than once, to their great pleasure, the last time for six weeks.

"But that was almost a year ago, madam, and we haven't heard from him since. Exactly ten months. Strange," he added, "because he forgot to settle his bill with us before he left."

She showed him a photo of Kristjan to be sure that they were talking about the same man.

He nodded.

"Six weeks is a long time at this hotel," he said. "It was most unlike Mr. Benediktsson to forget to settle up. We're worried about him. So we made inquiries at most of the other hotels in the city. Without success," he added after a moment's silence. "Unfortunately."

She thanked him for his help.

"Are you related?" he asked then.

She put the picture back in her bag.

"This is a beautiful hotel," she said and took her leave.

The church bell tolled twelve, her mind echoing the lazy strokes. To the south a skyscraper split the blue haze in two. People moved slowly, looking for shelter in the shade, wilting on benches under the trees. The odd person whistled a tune under his breath, with long pauses between the notes. Elisabet walked from one hotel to the next, along Fifth Avenue and down the side streets until she reached Central Park with its brilliantly colored flower beds. She made no progress.

After a week she finally swallowed her pride and went to see the Icelandic commercial attaché, Jon Sivertsen. It was one thing to ask unknown foreigners about her husband's whereabouts, another to ask a countryman. But she was desperate. It was hot. And the walls of the buildings were closing in on her.

He received her kindly. He simply nodded when she said: "My husband is lost." There was an Icelandic painting above the sofa where he sat. Horses in a snowstorm. He spoke quietly.

He said her husband had never had much to do with his countrymen in New York. He was unusual in this respect, because Icelanders generally stuck together. No doubt Kristjan had made friends in the city. He was, of course, popular wherever he went.

"That's not to say we didn't get on. Quite the contrary. He sometimes invited me to lunch and never let me pay. However hard I tried. A generous man, your husband, everyone knows that. But he goes his own way and doesn't need us."

He grew uncomfortable when she asked whether he thought Kristjan's agent could help her. She had a piece of paper with his name on it. "Andrew B. Jones," it said. She had rung his office but was told that he was away on business. Jon Sivertsen knew the name, nodded, fiddled with the ashtray on the table in front of him, moving it an inch away, then pulling it back towards him.

"It's a while since they stopped doing business together," he said eventually. "I don't know what happened, but business is business, you know." He smiled. "All sorts of things can happen in that game, as you can imagine. And on top of that, there's far less going on here for us since the war ended. I expect your husband has turned his attention back to Europe."

Horses in a snowstorm. The snow had drifted over their hoofprints but in the distance the faint shapes of mountains could be seen looming over them. The wind seemed to be picking up.

She stood and thanked him.

"I'm sorry not to have been able to help you," he said.

She smiled. "It was nice to see the horses," she said. "And the mountains, too."

He was confused for a moment, then realized she had been looking at the picture behind him.

As they walked to the door he vacillated, wondering whether he should mention the rumors. He took the door handle and stood still while he pondered, not opening the door until he had concluded that it would be doing her no favors. He himself had never seen Kristjan with the woman and for all he knew it might have been a brief fling. Two men said they had seen Kristjan with a woman at a nightclub, but from their description it was unclear whether it had been the same woman both times. And one of them had always been unreliable.

He opened the door. She left. He realized he felt almost like a servant in her presence. And still she couldn't have been more unassuming.

"If there is anything I can do . . ."

She stood still on the sidewalk outside. The avenue vanished into the haze, shimmering in the heat. She looked to the right, then the left.

Remained where she stood.

The plains behind, yellow fields and paddocks in the distance. She woke as the train was crossing a river; cattle wallowed in the channels, while farther down the current was stronger and the sand was red on the banks.

The sky was a long way off and the swallows which flew downstream seemed to float beneath it; her gaze followed them until her lids drooped again and she slept.

Cousin Hans met her at Grand Forks station. Maria was with him; she ran to her mother and wouldn't leave her side. Einar had stayed behind at the farm with Hans's wife. Their own children were grown up, except for one teenage girl. There was a white church in the field. Beyond it cows were grazing.

Einar was out in the meadow when they arrived. He came up to her and she stroked his cheek.

"My boy," she said. "You're so brown."

The wind sent ripples over the field, the sky arched impossibly high over the farm, the church tower stretched humbly towards it, a long way from the Almighty.

At night the stars hung like cheerful lanterns in the sky. The meadows were blue in the moonlight, the stars mirrored in the pond below the farm. The mornings were long and white, but in the evenings the brightness dimmed imperceptibly, and suddenly it was dark.

Nobody asked about her trip to New York. They didn't need to. Even Maria was quiet.

"There's enough food for everyone," said her cousin. "Stay as long as you like."

"Perhaps a few weeks," she said. "In case . . ."

He dropped his eyes.

"Just in case we hear anything."

She played the organ in church. On Sundays there was a service at eleven. The congregation numbered between fifty and sixty; Hans preached in English but sometimes read aloud from the Icelandic Hymns of Passion. There was a great deal of singing and afterwards people drank coffee. The dogs fought outside in the yard, then sprawled in the sunshine.

As fall turned to winter, the goldenrod and cattail withered, the sunflower disappeared and the meadows turned a pale dun. The children went to school. They had both begun to speak English, but it was difficult to get Maria to leave her mother in the mornings. The first few days she cried, then she stopped but said in parting: "You won't be gone when I get home from school, will you?"

Einar refused to speak Icelandic unless forced to. His English got better by the day.

Elisabet knitted and embroidered; her cushions and panels were sold down at Grand Forks, along with her sweaters, woolen hats, and scarves. The money went towards the household expenses.

She sat at the window as she worked. Sometimes when she looked out and glimpsed the pond she thought she was back at Eyrarbakki. She even imagined she could hear the pounding of the surf on the shore and see ships entering the bay. If she closed her eyes, she could see a gull.

She received a letter from Uncle Tomas. He told her news of Katrin and the twins, and asked what was keeping her. He hinted that the man who bought the company had not paid on time and was claiming that the business was even more rocky than he had been told when he signed the contract.

"I don't know if you'll ever see another krona from this man," wrote Tomas. "Unfortunately, I suspect he is in the right. But I will still provide Katrin with the little allowance she needs to look after the house and the twins," he added. "When you come home you ought to consider reducing your expenses. It's a big house."

The goldenrod's baskets found their way into the panel she was embroidering, and the pale blue of the sky was also there. At the top stood the year: 1920. In the evenings Hans read aloud and the family sat and listened. Einar was drawn to Hans and stayed close to him. He woke at the same time as Hans in the mornings and went out with him at daybreak, down the slope to the barn. When they opened the doors, the warm smell of the animals greeted them.

Late in January she rose from a half-knitted sweater and went into the room she shared with Maria. She was alone in the house. She took out the bag in which she kept what was left of their money, counted it, then closed the bag again. Outside there was frost on the ground. Here and there a blade of grass poked through. There was ice on the pond, in some places pale with snow.

She was standing by the window when her cousin came in. He was alone.

"I've never been very good at arithmetic, cousin, but it seems to me that I can only afford to take one of the children home to Iceland with me."

He looked down at the sweater, which she had left on the chair by the window. The needles lay on top of it.

"Now?"

"On the next ship. I've already stayed too long. The twins . . ."

"You know I'd lend you the money if I could."

"Einar is happy with you. Happier than with me. I hope I'll be able to send for him soon. Unless . . ."

She hesitated, turning away from him. When she started shaking he took her in his arms.

"Forgive me," she said.

He held her gently, in silence.

"I don't dare part with Maria."

In the afternoon she walked down to the pond with Einar. The ice was like a mirror. They came to a stop on the bank; she pointed out to him some flowers frozen in the ice. Their petals had not lost their color, they looked as if they were stretching towards them, happily, as if towards a great source of light.

"My boy," she said, "how you've grown."

She took his hand.

"Let's go in, Mother," he said. "You're cold."

The train whistled as it set off. Hans waved with his left arm until it was gone, his right laid around Einar's shoulders. The column of steam left behind by the train rose straight up into the cold winter air and slowly dispersed.

Then there was silence.

This is how I see you in my mind's eye—

You're sitting at the piano in the living room, it's sunny outside. Einar comes in, you look up to greet him. How old would he be now, I ask myself from habit. Twenty-eight, if I'm not mistaken. Twenty-eight years old, imagine! The years run together in a single thread and I forget what came first and what happened later. He looks like me—yes, in fact I see myself as a young man as he puts down his briefcase in the hall and takes off his light-colored coat. Why should he be carrying a briefcase? I can't explain it. But I'm always relieved by the sight of it.

You, on the other hand, have not changed. You're always the same. It's strange when I see Einar go over to you: you as you were when we first met, he a full-grown man. In earlier versions you are playing Mozart on the piano, but now I've managed to break free of him. I succeeded in the end. It wasn't easy. Now I see your fingers gently stroking the keys (I remember it always seemed as if you hardly needed to touch them), but all I can hear is the sound of a bird singing in the garden. "*Tschik, tschik.*" A wagtail, I guess.

I expect the twins are upstairs. There's no way I can conjure up a picture of them and I no longer look at the photo in the drawer as often as I used to. It confuses me. Puts time out of joint.

Maria is wearing a red summer dress. I see her cheek, faintly, as if in a mirror. She is fair, with shoulder-length hair. Delicately built like you, but taller. She is on her way downstairs when Einar comes in. The light streams towards her when he opens the door. She vanishes in the brightness and I lose sight of her.

That's how I picture you for myself. Sometimes while I'm awake. Sometimes in a dream.

Always the same.

Mack came riding up the slope, reined in at the top of the drive, then turned and looked out to sea. The afternoon sun shimmered above the waves, the horse's sweating flanks seeming to catch fire in its rays.

I watched him for a moment, then went inside, through the cool rooms, glancing briefly into the kitchen before going upstairs. Mack was still in the same place when I left, his reins hanging slack, his horse bowing its head.

In the kitchen the staff's evening meal of soup and veal was being prepared. They had begun to ladle the soup into bowls. It was green, the bowls blue. But I continued on up the stairs because Mack had invited me to dine with him. He had little to say when he arrived just after midday, seeming more serious than usual, even preoccupied. When I said jokingly: "I expect you'd like to stay in the golden suite again," he did smile slightly but made no reply. I hoped that whatever was troubling him would be dispelled by his ride over the hills.

The picture of the wheatear was lying on the desk in my room where I'd left it, half-finished. I'd completed the white rump and ochre breast, but its back, tail, and head still remained. However, there were no birds to be seen when I sat down in my chair on the balcony; at this time of day they seem to disappear in the endless sky, but when the blue twilight falls they return, perching on trees and bushes, silent as if contemplating the things they've witnessed on their journey through the sky.

At six the boy arrived and began to wash down the stones of the terrace. The trickling sound of the water soothed me and before I knew it my eyelids drooped and I fell into a doze. Yet I didn't completely lose awareness; I heard him finish the job and turn off the water. His movements were gentle and unhurried, his footsteps died away slowly as he dragged the hose round the corner. Then dusk fell and the sky descended to earth once more.

The Chief and Miss Davies are due next week. It's three months since they were here last. Unfortunately, Miss Davies' latest film received no better reviews than her previous effort, so I doubt they will be in high spirits when they arrive. I'll make sure that there is no alcohol concealed anywhere in the house.

I sat up in my chair when I heard footsteps on the path below. The lanterns had been lit. I must have dropped off; at least I wasn't sure where I was when I opened my eyes. It was Mack coming in through the back door, still in his riding boots, taking off his hat and rubbing his hand over his head. Lights shone from the kitchen windows, accompanied by the aroma of woodsmoke and roasting meat; I heard him greet someone as the door banged shut behind him. He was well liked by the people in the house.

When he had gone, I reverted to my old game and imagined his footprints steaming up from the terrace, brining me a clue as to what he had been thinking about. Yet for some reason I was none the wiser. This surprised me as generally I can invent something, at least spin myself a yarn, hazard a few guesses. But Mack left nothing behind him but silence.

We dined in a small room off the kitchen, with a view to the south over the ridges and valleys. The last vestiges of daylight faded on the peaks of the mountains and their outlines vanished like a smudged pencil stroke. I told the maids we didn't require their help—I would take care of serving and clear away myself. It was obvious that Mack didn't want us to be disturbed. We watched the changing hues of the scenery, the meeting between light and darkness, until the sun finally set and the spectacle was at an end.

"Magnificent," he said at last.

"Yes," I agreed, "there's no denying."

"How long have you been here, Christian?"

I wasn't surprised by the question, but had to pause and do some mental arithmetic before I could answer.

"Sixteen years."

"Sixteen years, well I'll be damned."

"I came here in 'twenty-one. In the summer."

"That early?"

"Yes, the first summer he stayed in the houses here on the hill. Work had hardly started on the main building."

"There've been a lot of changes since you first came here."

"You could say so."

"Have you often had your differences?"

"I'm sorry?"

"You and the Chief."

I replied that Mr. Hearst had a short temper but that we had always got on well, all the same.

"He's never threatened to fire you?"

"Fire me?"

"When he's lost his temper . . ."

"Yes, I suppose he has done that once or twice. But he cooled off and didn't mention it again. Behaved as if nothing had happened. It's many years ago now," I added.

Mack seemed relieved. Finally he smiled and sipped his wine. I had begun to wonder whether he was ever going to touch it.

"Strange man," he said then. "I was with him the day before yesterday in Los Angeles. He was in a bad mood. Miss Davies' latest movie looks like a flop. He's taking it hard. She was nowhere to be seen. She didn't need this. It's her fourth failure in a row. The old man was grumbling about everything. I had some things to go over with him—I'd put them down on paper so we could get it over and done with quickly, but he didn't listen to a word I said. What do you think he wanted to talk about instead?"

I said I couldn't begin to guess.

"Some rose he says was stolen from the hill here months ago. He reckoned he'd found a bush with a rose missing. Said he'd discussed it with you and told you to find the culprit. And what do you know?"

"What?"

"He says you lied to him."

Silence.

Mack burst out laughing.

"He said he'd found out that you had discovered the villain and hidden the fact from him. Some kid who works for one of his papers and was a guest up here. Of course, the kid didn't have the sense to keep his mouth shut, so the story got out and the old man realized that people were making fun of him. He told me to fire you."

I rose to my feet and prepared to clear away the dishes.

"Can I offer you some more meat?" I asked.

"Told me to fire you the moment he knew I was on my way here. Couldn't wait till next week when he's coming here himself. There was no way I could make him change his mind and I've been worried sick ever since. But I feel better now. He'll get over it like before. You'll see. It'll be forgotten when he comes here next week."

He retired early. I heard him whistling as he went upstairs. I myself stayed up for a long time.

They arrive tomorrow.

Since Mack left five days ago, I've been busy in my room early in the mornings and late at night. There are so many bits and pieces one collects over the years. I have absolutely no recollection of some of the things I find on shelves or in cupboards: magazine articles and newspaper clippings, all kinds of birds' feathers that I picked up when I first came here. I remember how exotic I found some of them—in color, flight, and behavior—and I had trouble fixing them on paper during those first months, even though I had them before my eyes most days. I remember once I had been watching a hummingbird for weeks, but when I sat down to draw it, all that emerged from my pencil was a meadow pipit. I was taken aback. I hadn't set eyes on one for years.

I realized just now when I pulled out my desk drawer and happened to glance out of the open window that I have never described my room to you. I picked up the letters I had written— I had no idea there were so many until I took them out of the drawer—and leafed through a few to check if I'd remembered right. No, it was just as I thought, I had never put in writing anything about my apartment, the room I've grown fond of after all these years. I don't know whether I was surprised; often one forgets the things that are closest. From my first day here on the hill, this room has provided me with a refuge and, if you can say this about a room, been a dear companion.

It's not a big room, fifteen by twenty feet at most, but it contains everything that matters to me. The things I brought from home are either here in the desk or in the drawer of the bedside table. Once I kept the boat that Einar had carved and painted blue up on my shelf, but I put it away in a drawer the day Miss Davies asked me about it. I remember being flustered and ending the conversation as quickly as I could; though there's no doubt she formed her own ideas.

The bed is against the northern wall, the balcony to the east, my desk opposite the bed, bookshelves between, and a chest of drawers by the door, which faces west. The windows are tall, reaching almost down to the floor. You can open both sides and I often do so when my room is stuffy. The balcony door has a glass panel. It's a bright room.

The furniture is of good quality, though unassuming. The bed and desk made from some red wood, the chest and bookshelf darker. Above the chest is an old map of Cairo that I long meant to take down, then changed my mind after I dreamed about the city one night.

I saw a cloud approaching over a pale desert; when it drew near it changed color, turning red and green, before dispersing into a thousand wings. The birds flew silently towards an open square in the heart of the city. When they alighted, they turned into flowers. I forced my way through the throng (the people were speaking loudly in some foreign tongue), pulled one of them up and examined it. It was hot. Its petals were soft and downy. I felt its heart beating in my palm. When I raised it to my face I awoke.

For a moment I felt a deep sense of bliss before the dream released me. I had touched beauty.

I have never dreamed this dream again. Yet often when I go to bed I try to recall what sort of mood I was in when I lay down to rest that evening. Then I lie still in the twilight, the picture hidden on the wall, the desert cold under white starlight. But I haven't found my way back there yet and know it is highly unlikely that I ever will.

Sometimes I'm awakened by the light in the mornings, sometimes by birdsong, sometimes by a din in the kitchen or footsteps on the terrace below. There's a rustling in the forest, a gust of wind wakes the leaves. I stretch, receiving the dawn through the open window. If I'm lucky this might be one of my good days.

Yes, it's strange that it's never occurred to me to describe my room before, seeing as I've become so fond of it. Strange I should do so only now, when I'm beginning to suspect I won't be here forever.

The car came up the hill later than expected; it was nearly four. I went to meet it, stopping as usual a few steps short and waiting for the chauffeur to get out and open the doors for them. I saw the Chief's white head through the window, he was looking in the other direction.

Miss Davies got out first. She walked over to me. She looked unusually frail. He remained sitting in the car.

"Come with me," she said and put her arm through mine.

"Shouldn't I take the baggage first?" I asked.

"It can wait. Let's go inside."

I looked round as we walked up the steps to the lower terrace. He was still in the car. The chauffeur was standing by the rear door.

"So," she said as we entered. "You look well."

I didn't answer, but nodded in thanks, if I remember right. She was rather pale and weary, so I couldn't return the praise.

She asked me to wait while she went to her room and cleaned off the dust from the journey, as she expressed it. When she returned she had removed her hat and applied some scent. She'd also had a nip of spirits. She could tell I knew.

"It was a long journey," she said, with the emphasis on *long*. "I was afraid you wouldn't be here when we arrived. Did Mack talk to you?"

I told her we'd talked.

"About the rose?"

"Yes, he mentioned the rose."

"And?"

"He said the Chief wanted to fire me."

She sighed. Helena came and jumped up at her. She scratched the dachshund behind the ears, then pushed her away.

"It's all my fault," she said. "He's been impossible ever since they started showing that damned movie. Do you know what the reviews have been like?"

I didn't answer.

"Fair," she said. "I'm awful and it's a terrible movie. But he doesn't understand. He thinks everyone's got it in for us."

"When should I leave?"

"Stop it. You're not going anywhere. He just got mad. He's still sore, but it'll wear off in a couple of days. The mountain air always has a good effect on him. Maybe you should ride out with him tomorrow morning," she said after a pause. "I'll suggest it to him."

I thanked her.

"We've got enough problems," she said. "I don't want any upsets here. By the way," she added as I was about to leave her. "The silver. I bought it back. It's going to be delivered today. To your attention. Bring it out when you set the table tonight. And don't say anything about me buying it. That's our secret."

She stayed behind when I went outside. The Chief had come in and gone up to his room. Helena followed me. She was lazy in the heat and lay down in the shade under a tree. For some reason my conversation with Miss Davies had failed to ease my mind.

———

I didn't see him until at the dinner table. Earlier in the day he had summoned the chef and given him his orders for the menu. He usually consulted me, so the chef was taken aback when he was summoned alone. He was nervous.

"What do you suppose he wants?" he asked me.

"Food," I replied.

The old man seemed puzzled when he came down to the dining room. He paused in the doorway and looked round before sitting down. At first I thought he hadn't expected to see me, then I realized he was looking for Miss Davies. He shot a glance at the clock, then sat staring ahead in silence.

I stood motionless. We were alone together in the room. The table seemed larger than before; he looked tiny in his chair beside it. He reached out for the ketchup bottle in front of him, turned it so he could read the label, waited. If he noticed the silver, he didn't mention it. I hadn't expected him to.

"Where is she?" he said to himself, without looking at me.

"I'll go look," I said.

She walked into the room just as I reached the door. She was unsteady on her feet. Clearly she had been drinking after I left her. I led her to the table. She sat down without a word. She hadn't changed for dinner. It was very unlike her, and it made me uneasy.

I hadn't seen him this depressed since the plane crash. There was misery in his eyes when he looked at her, yet he said nothing. It was she who began to talk.

"You'd be much happier if you were rid of me. I'm nothing but trouble. So it's best I go. We're not even married, so it wouldn't have any"—she searched for the word—"consequences. No consequences."

"Marion!"

I had never heard her talk this way before. Never heard her mention one word about the fact that they weren't married. My heart sank listening to her.

He stood up and reached across the table for her hand.

"You must eat. Where's the food?" he asked loudly.

I hurried out to the kitchen. He was standing over her when I returned, trying to calm her down. Unsuccessfully, it seemed. Her tone was mocking.

"You can't live with a woman you can't even have a child with. These endless abortions. Hard for you. It must be so hard to be with a woman who's so . . . What was the word you used—careless? I should have written it down so I wouldn't forget . . ."

She finally stopped, but didn't touch her food. Just sat in silence, watching him trying to eat. He had no appetite. I invented a reason to leave the room. I saw he was relieved when I went.

It's a mystery to me why he took her into the projection room after dinner.

"I really want to watch it with you," I heard him say. "It'll make you feel better. Such a wonderful movie. You've never looked more beautiful."

"No," she said. "Please."

"Come on, take my hand."

I looked in on them half an hour later. They sat in darkness, images flickering on the screen in front of them, his head sometimes illuminated, sometimes in shadow. She sat slumped at his side.

Ever Since Eve, the movie was called. She played a stenographer who becomes tired of men chasing her and goes into disguise as an ugly duckling. In the end, the man she loves discovers her natural beauty and marries her.

"Look at that," he said and nudged her. "That was terrific."

I thought at first that she was asleep, then heard the gasping sobs.

"Stop it," she begged, "stop the picture . . . you fool . . . I can't . . ."

I hurried away.

I had a hell of a time getting to sleep that night. Everything seemed to be collapsing. The waning moon cast a thin light into my room and when the leaves of the palm trees brushed against the wall it was as if someone was breathing outside the window. They had retired early; I left my door open in case anyone called me.

When I got out of bed I thought I'd probably misheard. The wind had picked up outside and the branches of the trees beat against the wall from time to time as if their hearts were heavy. The moon threw their moving images onto the floor and up the wall; there was wildness in the weather. Nevertheless, I thought I heard a crash somewhere in the house, and pulled on my pants and undershirt before going out into the passage. The door to their suite was shut, so I turned and went downstairs. The faint luminescence of the wall lamps lit my way—the moonlight couldn't penetrate this far. I heard footsteps and paused, then realized it was the echo of my own feet.

I checked first whether anyone had left a window open in the kitchen or pantry, then headed straight for the reception rooms. It was as if something was pulling me, some force I didn't understand.

She lay on the floor by the terrace door. She was wearing a white silk robe; the moonlight enveloped her and the shadows of the trees raged over her like wild beasts. It seemed likely that she'd been on her way outside; her hand was stretched out towards the door. She was deathly pale, with foam at the corners of her mouth. I bent and lifted her head, it was heavy, her body limp. I felt a weak heartbeat.

By the time the doctor arrived, it had started to rain. I was waiting for him by the main entrance. He wore a dark overcoat that was already drenched when he reached the house. I helped him out of the coat. He looked me in the eye.

"Upstairs," I said.

I had carried her there. She was light. I'd never realized how delicately built she was; it was like carrying a bird.

I laid her on her bed before alerting the Chief. When he had rubbed the sleep from his eyes, I could see nothing in them but pain.

"I've called the doctor," I said. "I'll wait for him downstairs."

I hurried away. Behind me I heard his footsteps as he went into her room. I thought I heard him say: "Marion, what have you done?" but paused on the staircase when he repeated the words: "Marion, what have I done?"

The doctor's shoes were wet. He left damp footprints along the passageway. I waited outside while he went into her room.

I heard her retching. They called me. I ran downstairs to get a bowl. She was slumped on the floor by the toilet, the doctor holding her head. I wet a towel and washed her face, then helped her back into bed. She opened her eyes once, tried to raise her hand to touch my cheek but couldn't manage it. I left the room again. The doctor stayed with her for twenty minutes. He came out alone. I escorted him downstairs.

"That was a close call," he said. "Where was she when you found her?"

I told him.

"And the pills?"

"They were in her room."

"She didn't have them with her?"

"No, the bottle was on her bedside table, empty."

"It was a very narrow escape," he said. "If you hadn't . . ."

He fell silent and I helped him into his coat, then put on my boots and fetched an umbrella.

"It's still raining," he commented.

We went outside.

"You don't need to come with me," he said. "You'll only get soaked too."

I went with him. The sea was audible in the distance. We walked towards the headlights of the car, which was waiting for him. The rain poured down. The lights flickered in the sheets of water.

"They'll come and fetch her in the morning," he said. "When she's awake."

I stood still and watched the car retreating down the hill. The wind had dropped and I lowered the umbrella. My feet were already wet and now the rest of me became drenched in seconds. The rain was warm and gentle; it felt good on my forehead.

They didn't leave in the morning because she slept till midday. He held her hand as they went down the stairs. I followed a little behind. She tried to smile at me. I meant to smile back, but by then strange tremors had seized the corners of her mouth.

They vanished into the bright afternoon and I was left behind wondering whether it really had been a smile that trembled for an instant on her lips.

There is a corner of the soul where the shadows dwell. Most days they keep to their place, and if I sense that they're about to emerge I try to take precautions before they can invade my consciousness. I dip my hands in cold water and splash my face; it's like extinguishing a fire.

Sometimes I conjure up a picture of you to ease my mind. You're sitting at the piano in the living room, Einar is coming in. You haven't changed.

The clouds are high in the sky today and the sun shines uninterrupted. The bell in the campanile clangs out of time; the repairmen are due tomorrow. When I passed the indoor swimming pool earlier I noticed an empty glass laying on the edge. I have no idea who left it there; I don't remember seeing it there yesterday. When I bent down to pick it up I caught sight of my face reflected on the surface of the water. It was as if it had always been there, floating among the gilded sea lions of the ceiling. I started when it stared back at me. The shadows had emerged from their hiding place.

Drip, drop. Steam rises from the hot pool and condenses on the ceiling, then falls into the water again. One drop at a time, I can count up to five between them. The sound echoes in the house, the blue walls are cold to the touch, silently waiting for me to move on so that they can echo my footsteps. I look up, unable to stare into the water any longer. When I leave I suspect that my face is still there, floating amid the sea lions.

You haven't changed. Einar is coming in; I know it's him, though I have difficulty picturing him in my mind. When I try, I invariably see myself as a young man.

A gust sweeps over the hill, taking the cypress by surprise, as the day has been calm for the most part. It sways and seems unsteady for a moment, then recovers and captures the wind after a brief struggle. Somewhere in its leaves raindrops have remained concealed from the night before but now are shaken free. The wind drops again, biding its time.

The picture vanishes. Darkness falls on it, subjugating my mind and depriving me of sight. You are no longer in the living room, there is no one in the living room and no one opens the front door and says: "Hello, it's only me! I'm home!" No one comes down the stairs in a red dress and vanishes in the brightness that floods in through the door. No one, nothing. There is nothing before my eyes but darkness.

Yet I can hear whispering. You're on a street in Reykjavik, people are watching you and putting their heads together. You know they're there but hurry away without looking at them, moving closer to the walls of the buildings with their concealing shadows. But the voices pursue you, you can't drive them away, even though you quicken your pace and begin to hum a tune. "There she is . . . the wife of that man who vanished. I wonder where he went. Some people think he drowned himself . . . Or went abroad, taking all their money . . . Four children, imagine! The poor little mites . . ."

The whispering echoes in my head, accompanied by the tune

you're singing to try to drown it out. It's as if someone keeps turning up the volume of a radio; I can't turn it down, and in the end I take to my heels to try to outrun it, clasping my hands over my ears.

I feel as if I'm going mad.

Last night I dreamed I had left my shadow on Maria's bed. And my soul was left behind with the shadow.

I come to a stop, my heart pounding in my chest. It's hot, the sweat is pouring down my face. Push aside your troubles, that's what I've always told myself, try to forget, only think about things that soothe your mind. And I managed it most days, while everything was fine up here on the hill. But now the stage has begun to crumble and there is a menacing silence all around me.

An illusion, I tell myself now, nothing but an illusion. Yet I've managed to keep it alive all these years.

The bell in the campanile strikes the half-hour.

The random clanging of the bell fills me with misgiving, though there's no reason why it should. Sometimes it doesn't strike for hours on end, then tries to make up for it by ringing incessantly. "Can't you get here today?" I asked the repairman when I phoned him this morning. "Today," I repeated. I think he was surprised by the urgency in my voice.

"Tomorrow at the earliest," he replied.

There was nothing I could do.

The half-hour.

I carry on up the slope, past the cypress tree, without using it for support, without using anything for support. "Christian!" someone calls, but I don't answer. I don't stop to catch my breath until I enter the house, don't wipe the sweat from my brow, hurry straight up to my room.

The balcony door is open. I'm hot but don't take off my jacket.

A fly buzzes in the window. I hasten to open the desk drawer, certain of finding comfort in the letters I've been writing to you. I reach out for them but they have an alien appearance all of a sudden, as if I hadn't written them. My hands, usually steady, now begin to shake. When I go to put the letters down I have to grab the edge of the desk to stop myself falling. I feel dizzy. The letters fall to the floor.

"Am I coming down with something?" I ask myself. My forehead feels hot.

The words I've been searching for. I know they won't do you any good, yet I still keep trying to find them.

My heartbeat slows gradually and I stoop to pick up the letters. Just now I was ready to throw them away, but I've changed my mind. I put them back in the desk, in an old shoebox with various other odds and ends of sentimental value: feathers, old keys, a few pebbles, the photographs I've held on to. I decide to tidy up the desk and the shelves, as well, throw away all sorts of unnecessary stuff I've accumulated over the years. I may regret some things in the act of throwing them away, but they'll be forgotten a moment later. Perhaps I'll pick out a few bird drawings, but not many of them are worth hanging on to. I'm sure I'll feel better once I'm done. I read in a magazine the other day that tidying your home helps to clear your mind.

I'm going to try to finish my clear-out before it gets dark and the boy starts washing down the terrace under my balcony. I want to sit out there and welcome the dusk. I'm sure the clouds in my mind will disperse, the despair will loosen its grip on me and the darkness retreat.

I'll never send the letters, I told myself a moment ago. But now I feel optimistic that I'll change my mind after a good rest.

I didn't sleep badly. When I awoke, my despondency had largely lifted; the dawn had finally driven the shadows back into their corner. I'd been getting desperate; it had seemed as if they were never going to leave during these past few days. All the same, I lay still for a while, just to make sure, staring up at the ceiling, then gradually looking around me; it's strange how sharp the eye becomes when the clouds disperse in one's soul, it's like looking through clear air after heavy rain.

"Well, look at that," I said to myself. I had forgotten that the doorframe was carved down to the floor. Then a long body shook itself in the passage, a collar jingled, and I got out of bed to pat Helena and greet the new day.

It was nearly three and the lunch tray with its dirty dishes was still lying on the table, attracting flies. He hadn't rung for me, so I knocked at his door to find out if he needed anything.

"Who's that whistling?" he asked when I opened the door.

"I'm sorry?"

"There was someone whistling outside. I heard it yesterday evening, too."

I said I didn't know.

A week has passed since he took Miss Davies to the sanatorium. He has been staying near her in a hotel. He came home yesterday evening and is going back to her tomorrow.

"First I thought it was a bird, then I realized it must be someone whistling. Like this," he said and tried to reproduce the sound.

I think he knew I wasn't telling the truth. He knew, too, why I wouldn't enlighten him about the boy who whistled to keep himself happy. So he added:

"It raises the spirits to hear that whistling. I could do with that, Christian, I certainly could do with that."

He's making peace, I told myself. Well, I never. I guess he must have thought a good while before coming up with the whistle as an excuse for conversation and now he's trying to smile. He's weary. Yet there's a gleam of hope in his eyes.

"Shouldn't I take the tray? The flies . . ."

"She's feeling better," he said. "The sea air's good for her. Yesterday we went for a long walk on the beach. I . . ."

"Please send her my regards," I said.

"I can never thank you enough, Christian. It could have gone very differently."

"I hope she'll feel better soon."

"She's always had a soft spot for you, Christian. She trusts you."

Outside somebody was whistling.

"There," he said. "Do you hear?"

I nodded but stood motionless, without putting down the tray.

"What tune would that be?"

"Probably just something he made up," I said.

"It raises the spirits. Yes, really raises the spirits."

Silence.

"Was there anything else?"

"No, nothing else."

I was about to leave, but hesitated for a moment as it was obvious that he wanted to say something to me. Just as I was about to turn my back and walk out, he cleared his throat.

"Christian, do you think . . . ? You found her. You do think it was an accident, don't you?"

I was still holding the tray. I was on the point of answering him honestly, rather than shielding him from the truth yet again, when he continued:

"As she was coming round she asked about a note. Over and over again. 'The note,' she said. 'Don't read the note. Where is it? I must have it.' Do you have any idea what she was talking about? She wasn't holding a note when you brought her upstairs, but there was ink on her fingers. On her left hand. I don't understand it."

When I found her she was clutching a white piece of paper in her left hand. Her hand was damp with cold sweat and the ink had begun to run. I loosened her fingers, folded the note, and put it in my pocket. Wiped the foam from her mouth and kissed her. First on the brow, then on the mouth. Lightly. The note contained only a few words. I expect I could have made them out if I'd tried. But I threw it on the fire as soon as I had said goodbye to the doctor that night, went straight into the kitchen and tossed it into the embers on the hearth.

"No," I said at last. "I didn't find any note. She must have been delirious when she came round."

"I thought so," he said, like a man who has received good news after a worrying medical examination and can't hold back the flood of words. "I knew it must have been like that. 'Kiss me again,' she said to me before she began talking about the note. 'Kiss me again.' It meant a lot to me to hear her say that," he added, looking almost shy. "It was just an accident. She could do with the rest, that's for sure."

I agreed.

"Anything else?" I asked then.

"No, nothing else. Thank you, Christian. Thank you."

I felt his eyes on me as I went to the door.

Some people claim they can tell from the smell what kind of wood is burning. I myself recognize the redolence of laurel when fire has taken hold of it, and I've always been rather surprised that lavender doesn't smell better when it burns. The poppy and the aster wilt before the flames can get a grip; the heat which goes in advance fells them like scythes. It is laurel that has such a recognizable smell. I always enjoy the crackling of its branches when we throw it on the fire to flavor the meat.

The fire started during the afternoon in a ravine east of the hill. It had been hot and dry for the past few days and for once the fog hadn't crept up onto land, pooling instead down on the coast on the few nights when it had made an appearance. The slopes were yellow and the grass stiff, the wind shrill in its blades.

The ravine was deep and when the smoke had risen high enough in the sky to be visible from the buildings, the flames had already begun to pour towards its mouth and climb the bare cliff walls inside. But by then the scent of burning laurel had already reached us; it was the head gardener who noticed it first, though he didn't know where it came from. He hailed me; we stood at the top of the hill in front of the main house, scanning the land-scape, unable to spot fire or smoke anywhere. There were still a few deer on the slopes, and when a group came bounding from the east, fleeing down towards the plain, we decided to ride in their direction.

We were only halfway to the ravine when the smoke finally cleared the ridge. It was blue and stood straight up in the air, bil-lowing over at the top like children doing somersaults.

We decided that the gardener should go home and get help while I went on. The blaze met me as I approached the ravine. Behind it the earth was piebald. At the top of the slope below the ravine stood a cluster of old oak trees; the fire was headed in their direction. Further down the slope the grass stood thick and tall. The fire caught hold in one place and simultaneously sprang up in another, writhing along the ground like a snake and shooting up every tree in its course, yellow in one place, blue in others, red at its heart, black at its edges. I rode up to it, felt its fury. When I sensed my eyebrows singeing, I backed off.

Thirty of us set out to battle against it. We split up, the head gar-dener leading one team, I the other. The fire engine rolled back and forth along the tracks which had been laid the year before last, but they ended far from where the fire was burning. We formed a chain, passing along water in buckets, and the fire laughed at us. We did delay its spread to some degree, but when darkness began to fall and I looked back over the way we had come, I saw that we had been in constant retreat since the struggle began. Where we had originally taken up our stand there was now scorched earth.

East of the ravine was a belt of gravel which extended straight across the hillside below, so the only direction the fire could take was towards the buildings on the hill. We were joined by rein-forcements from the village as the day wore on, but at the same time men were dropping out of our ranks. There were forty of us at most, but not for long.

When it grew dark accidents began to happen, one after another. Those who had been at it longest were exhausted, some didn't watch where they put their feet and two were caught unawares by the fire hiding itself in pockets and flaring up from the ashes where no spark seemed to remain, while others inhaled smoke and were forced to leave. The doctor had taken part in the fight, but now had more than enough to do tending the injured.

The previous day the Chief had gone to visit Miss Davies at the sanatorium, but the head gardener had phoned him before we began to fight the fire. The old man had always been fond of the oak trees and now urged us to save them if we could. The head gardener told him the buildings could be in danger. He decided to start for home without delay. I reckoned he would arrive just after midnight.

There wasn't a breath of wind. The fire gathered strength in the darkness and seemed to tower higher than ever. When I approached, it reared over me. As I looked up, it took my shadow and hurled it to the ground behind me.

Midway between the fire and the buildings on the hill there was a dry riverbed. The head gardener and I conferred and concluded that our only hope was to try to arrest the blaze there. In some places the riverbed was so wide that the flames wouldn't be able to reach the vegetation on the other side, but in two places it entered a narrow defile where the distance between the banks was short. We decided to send most of our force there to tear up the laurels on either side and spread sand over the grass. Ten men remained behind and continued pouring water onto the flames to slow their advance.

I wasn't aware of feeling tired. Something was driving me on, some rage which took me by surprise. I advanced furthest of all the men into the tongues of flame and was the last to retreat. The head gardener twice yelled at me to take care. I glanced over at him to show I'd heard, but took no heed of his words.

Every now and then I felt a swish of air as birds fled the conflagration in the darkness. They were flying to the sea. I looked up and saw that the smoke had hidden the stars.

Midnight was approaching when the fire reached the riverbed. We had filled all the buckets with water and lined them up along the banks up the slope, and stood now side by side, silently waiting. Faces glowed. Some looked away. I stood towards the top of the line at the steep point where the riverbed was narrowest. We had spread gravel and sand on the banks on both sides and dampened the earth. But it was still hot and the water quickly evaporated. I looked over my shoulder. Lights were on in the buildings as if nothing had happened. I thought I saw a car driving up the hill.

The fire didn't just seek one or two spots to attempt a crossing, but attacked in five places at once. Where it found a foothold I can't imagine because no one had seen anything but dirt, stones, and gravel in the places where it now shot up. In some places it swiftly died down, but in others it grew in power with every inch it gained on us. Where we had broadened the riverbed, the sand was burning. The fire leaped towards me as if goading me.

It got across in three places at once. Where I stood there were only five of us, but further down the head gardener had twenty men helping him. The fire was stronger there and burned over a wider area. The boy who washes down the terrace in the evenings suddenly appeared. For some reason this seemed a good omen. I took him with me up the hillside.

I don't know how long the battle lasted. I had long since lost the sense of time. We had stripped to the waist and while three men ran to fetch water, two of us stood and beat the earth with our shirts and jackets. Although the fire had got across and taken hold on our side, we had managed to slow its passage.

I waded into the flames, beating the earth. It was as if I were standing to one side, watching myself charging into the fire. I felt the heat on my body yet wasn't burned. My helpers stood behind me; once when I emerged from the flames, they splashed water over me. They had thought I was on fire. I told them not to waste water.

I have no explanation for my behavior. Later when I finally took thought for my skin, I saw that all the hairs on my chest and arms were singed, yet I had no burns anywhere.

Gradually the fire began to lose its grip, first at our position higher up the slope. When I was sure I could contain it alone, I told my helpers to go down and give the others a hand. They hesitated, saying they weren't sure it was sensible, the fire had tricked us before, flaring up just when we thought it was slackening. I assured them I could cope single-handed. "I'll call you if I need to," I promised. They went. I noticed that they kept looking back at me on their way down the slope.

The flames stopped a few yards from the bank. They had spread downwards at first when their way was barred, then up the slope, but now they gradually lost momentum and sank, one after the other, into the ash they had created. I was hard pushed, but there was now no doubt of the outcome.

Finally the moon appeared, a crescent in the eastern sky. When I smothered the last spark, I was abruptly engulfed in darkness. I was taken unawares and my eyes took a long time to adjust after the bright glare.

Victory whoops sounded from down below, where the men had gone in for the kill. They had formed a ring round the dying blaze and begun to sing. Their shadowy figures rose and fell against the glowing backdrop, taking to the air, leaving the earth behind.

Gradually the men began to drift off home. The head gardener had minor burns on his arms, so I urged him to get his wounds tended to while I made sure that the fire hadn't sprung up again anywhere else.

The ash crunched as I set off in the darkness. Its heat was welcome in the cooling night. I walked towards the moon, past the ravine where the fire had originated, across the gravel belt beyond and up the hillside. I didn't look over my shoulder until I paused in a hollow at the top of the hill and looked back over the area where the fire had raged.

I was calm. It was as if the fire that had been burning inside me all these years was at last dying down.

The man in the photograph is cheerful and tanned. He's wearing a shirt, open at the neck, his thick hair combed back. He's on the left, the head gardener on the right, and the boy who washes down the terrace in the evenings stands between them. Behind them a cypress is visible in front of the main house. "Christian Benediktsson, Mr. Hearst's butler," says the caption below the picture, followed by the names of the others. "FOREST FIRE AT SAN SIMEON!" shouts the headline, "STAFF WIN BATTLE AGAINST BLAZE."

The Chief took the photo himself, the morning after the fire; Kristjan couldn't remember having seen him in such high spirits for a long time; he praised them to the skies, promising to pay a salvage award to all those who had taken part. Kristjan, however, hadn't realized that the Chief intended to publish the picture in his papers—he had wanted to take them by surprise.

It was only seven in the morning when the Chief banged on his door. Kristjan had already got up, been downstairs, and opened the door out onto his balcony. The Chief didn't usually wake up this early, but he had ordered an employee to drive from Los Angeles with an early copy of the paper so that he could personally present it to his butler.

"Is something wrong?" asked Kristjan when he opened the door.

The Chief entered and spread the paper on the desk.

"Front page," he said. "You deserve it."

The Chief wasn't surprised when Kristjan didn't seem over-joyed—his butler was not in the habit of showing his emotions—but he was a little taken aback when he didn't so much as smile.

"You fought like heroes," he said. "Who knows what would have happened . . ."

The front page. Kristjan ran his eyes down the article.

". . . Christian Benediktsson, William Randolph Hearst's but-ler, led the team of household staff along with head gardener, Nigel Keep. After battling the blaze for hours, they managed to halt the flames only a stone's throw from a grove of trees stand-ing right by Mr. Hearst's hilltop ranch . . ."

"The *Los Angeles Examiner*," muttered Kristjan at last, as if to himself.

The Chief adopted a portentous tone. "Not just the *Examiner*, Christian. Today when people wake up in Los Angeles, San Fran-cisco, Chicago, Boston, New York . . . when they get up, rub the sleep from their eyes, and sit down to their breakfast of coffee or tea, eggs and bacon, fruit juice, cornflakes . . . when they sit down and spread out the paper in front of them, you'll be the first thing they see. And they'll be all fired up, if I can put it like that, start the new day reassured that mankind can overcome any challenge. News like this puts heart into people, Christian. When they read stories like this they start to believe in themselves."

He had said what he came to say and seemed pleased with how it had gone, so he just clapped Kristjan on the shoulder as he left, asking him to make sure that the head gardener and others who might be interested in the news got to see the paper.

The next few days crept by. Kristjan was on edge during the daylight hours, slept little at night. Fortunately for him there was plenty to do—the Chief had decided to throw an extravagant party in honor of Miss Davies' homecoming; she was expected in just under two weeks' time. He had confided in Kristjan that he regarded the forest fire as marking a turning point in his life; recently he had had to retreat before one attack after another, but this attack had been repulsed and he had sensed when he came home that evening and saw the last flames extinguished in the distance that now the tide had turned.

"I don't believe in coincidences, Christian. It's time to take action. I've been waiting for this moment for a long while."

"A big party," he said. "A hundred guests. Like in the old days, Christian."

The first few days were slowest to pass, but when nothing happened, Kristjan's fears were gradually put to rest. Yet at times it was almost as if he wanted to be found, so that he could make a clean breast of things. But his eagerness faded when he couldn't answer what he meant by making a clean breast of things, and then the fear tightened its hold again, though he tried to immerse himself in the preparations for the party.

A week passed and he began to relax. One morning when he awoke he even thought he'd dreamed about the birds in the desert, but when he tried to recall his dream he realized that it had been wishful thinking. Yet he took it as a good omen, all the same.

Jon Sivertsen laid down the newspaper, took off his glasses and rubbed the bridge of his nose. The man in the photo had barely changed, though Jon didn't remember him being so tall. Perhaps it's just that the men beside him are short, he thought. Nigel Keep, head gardener. An unnamed houseboy. He put his glasses on again, stood up, and looked in the mirror. He was sure that he himself had changed more in the intervening years, his hair had thinned at the temples, the pounds piled on. And his sight hadn't improved either; the glasses were, unfortunately, brand-new. Kristjan doesn't look as though he's had too hard a time of it, he said to himself.

He sat down again and picked up the phone on his desk. It was four years since he'd received the letter from Hans Thorstensen of North Dakota asking him to let the sender know in the unlikely event that he should hear any news of Kristjan Benediktsson. He still had the letter, was mildly amused by it. Hans talked at great length about the weather, like any Icelandic farmer. He also relayed news of family members, both those Jon knew of and others he had never heard mentioned. This naïveté was refreshing in a city where people tended to be brusque and sarcastic. Perhaps I've been here too long, Jon remembered thinking to himself when he finished reading the letter.

He wasn't used to the glasses yet, taking them off and putting them on again before he made the call. His eyes fell on the painting on the wall opposite. He remembered as if it were yesterday the time she had come here to look for her husband.

Miss Davies was due on Thursday. It was now Tuesday.

The preparations for the party had gone better than expected. Tents had been erected on the terrace and in the gardens round the main house; the menu had been completed and the cooks were already making arrangements for the dinner—boning meat and trussing birds; a fleet of cars had been ordered to drive guests from the station at San Luis Obispo; around eighty people would be staying for the weekend. The Chief had decided to screen only movies starring Miss Davies; Kristjan was surprised when he consulted him about which movies he should show and was almost proud of himself for having had the courage to suggest *Show People,* though he knew it wasn't one of the old man's favorites.

"Do you really think so?" he'd asked. "*Show People?*"

"I'm sure it would make Miss Davies happy. She was very funny in it." And when the Chief nodded, he had plucked up the courage to add: "I think, if you don't mind my saying so, that it would be better to show only the movies that were well received."

The Chief nodded again.

"You're right, my friend. Yes, you're absolutely right."

Walking into the Night

When Kristjan received the letter that afternoon, he had been rushing around since the early morning. It was a long time since a party had been so eagerly awaited on the hill, by the staff just as much as the Chief. The old man didn't relax for a moment, summoning Kristjan several times a day to go over this and that, consulting him on various details, who should have which room, whether they should have a horseback trip on the program for Saturday, and so on. His main concern, however, was when he should tell Miss Davies about the party, because it couldn't be kept a secret once she arrived.

"Could we perhaps take down the tents before she arrives?" he asked, then shook his head without waiting for Kristjan's reply. "No, that won't work. Perhaps I'll tell her about it as we drive up the hill. When she catches sight of the tents. What do you think about that? Or perhaps I could blindfold her and have the band start playing in the tent in front of Casa Grande as soon as I take off her blindfold? Well, don't you think that's a good idea? What do you think, Christian, wouldn't that be perfect?"

Kristjan had just finished explaining this new plan to the band leader when the letter was handed to him. He didn't often get letters—no, it was a rare event, and then generally from people who'd been guests on the hill, wanting to thank him. But this wasn't a thank-you letter, they were slim affairs, written on small cards, a few lines; this envelope was bulky, the handwriting that of someone who was getting on in years. He was relieved to see that it wasn't Elisabet's writing, and this made him ashamed.

He was alone in the pantry when the boy brought him the letter and he stood still for a long while before looking at it. When he finally got up the nerve, he stuck the letter in his pocket and went up to his room. There he shut the door, sat down on his bed, and took out the envelope. He hesitated for a moment before he read the name of the sender: Hans Thorstensen, North Dakota. He recognized the name, and, carefully opening the envelope, began to read.

It's with mixed emotions that I take up my pen on this fine fall day to send you a few lines. You'll know the reason, though no doubt you'll wonder why I should be the one to get in touch with you. I assume you're ignorant of the fate of your family, unless you have made inquiries about them without their knowledge, which I find unlikely. I'm aware that I'm doing you no favors by writing to you. You would have got in touch with your family long ago if that had been your intention . . .

"Christian!" a voice called and he jumped. They were looking for him, the band wanted to rehearse the tunes they were to play when Miss Davies arrived and the band leader thought it safer to ask permission to play out on the terrace before they began. Kristjan laid the letter on his bed, went down and delayed his return upstairs, but in the end he could stay away no longer.

. . . I'm an old man now and use every spare moment I have to tie up any loose ends, as no one knows when the end might come. When we heard about the newspaper article, I suggested to your son Einar that he should get in touch with you himself. However, I was not surprised when he put off doing so, so I decided to write you myself.

Einar has lived with my wife and myself ever since he came to this country as a boy with his mother . . .

Kristjan sat on the bed and read. Hans was painstaking, leaving nothing out, taking his time. He wrote that he had learned his style from the Icelandic sagas, which he read every night before going to sleep. Outside the band played "You are my sunshine, my only sunshine."

Einar is married to a girl from an Icelandic family and they have two children, Hans and Elisabet. He took over the farm from me several years ago; he's a hard worker and down to earth, trustworthy, a man of few words but to the point, a good man. He has been like the best of sons to me . . .

Kristjan lost the thread, stared into space. The band continued to play the same tune over and over, louder each time, it seemed. The blaring of the trumpet echoed in his head along with the words which accompanied the tune: ". . . when skies are grey . . ."

Maria returned to Iceland with Elisabet, studied needlework—she has inher-

ited her mother's skill—and is now carrying her first child, having got married last summer . . . The twins . . .

He stood up but immediately sat down again, feeling faint. "Christian!" he heard someone calling far away, but the cries were drowned by the noise of the band, which struggled again and again with the same phrase, the drums like the pounding in his chest, "my sunshine, my only sunshine . . ." "Christian, where are you? Christian!" Carrying her first child . . . a fine man . . . the twins . . .

Elisabet died nearly five years ago. She had a peaceful end.

By the turn-off to the fishing village, a gray horse was standing under a tree. The day was hot, the sun at its zenith. Kristjan had been walking for over an hour. He had left the car where it would be easy to find; drove past the turn-off so that no one would guess he had headed that way, and parked next to a green shack where they sold fishing tackle.

The horse swung its head in his direction, then went back to grazing under the tree. He put down his satchel and canvas bag and walked over, stopping a couple of paces away so as not to alarm it. Its white back was mottled with the shadows of leaves, which hung unmoving in the noontime calm, and the silhouette of a bird hidden in the foliage—when it raised its wings, the leaves next to it stirred.

Kristjan put a hand to his brow to shade his eyes from the sun and peered up into the tree but couldn't see the bird anywhere.

The short stretch of road to the village ran down a descending series of hills, swinging to cross a stream in one place but otherwise straight. It was little used; Kristjan had been waiting for awhile with no sign of a car. He could see part of the village where it ran out at the foot of the slope, the canning factories and docks in front of them, the bay beyond. Gulls came screaming in from the sea ahead of ships heavily laden with sardines; they sailed out in the evenings and fished until morning.

In the note he left for the Chief, he wrote that he wasn't sure when he'd return. If anyone made inquiries after him, he asked the Chief to see that they were given a shoebox he had left behind containing a few small odds and ends, tied up with string. He wasn't sure why the string had seemed necessary. He had reorganized the contents of the box, adding the boat Einar had given him and leaving untouched the photographs, pebbles, and the swan's feather that his son had painted blue and presented to him as a bookmark. He doubted he would even remember it. But perhaps he'll remember the boat, he thought to himself, he took enough trouble over it.

I've asked Einar to come with me to visit you, Hans Thorstensen had written. *He's reluctant, I won't hide the fact from you, but I know he'll do it for me. I don't want to leave this world without having seen you two meet, and I know that this will not happen without my intervention. I'll call you beforehand on the telephone, although I abhor the contraption. Sooner rather than later, as I am not only old but in poor health as well. Yet I have nothing to complain of . . .*

Hans had phoned the previous morning; the guests were still asleep, having traveled up from Los Angeles overnight. Kristjan claimed he was busy and asked the operator to take a message. But he had made his decision before the phone rang, had been up all night packing his bags.

No one could have guessed during the party that he was short of sleep. He bustled around indoors and out, keeping an eye on everything, making sure that nothing went awry. The Chief was in top form, Miss Davies in the highest of spirits, and the guests seemed infected by their gaiety, singing and dancing till the early hours.

"I feel much better," Miss Davies told him when she arrived and the band had finished playing for her. "So much better, Christian." She had tried to have a word with him before the party but he made sure he was too busy, keen to avoid a longer conversation. He had already taken his leave of her.

He left when all the clearing up was done and everyone had gone to bed. Tatters had torn off the veils of fog that lay along the shore and when he drove down the hill they came sailing towards him, glowing white in the moonlight. Dawn was breaking in the east, the first glow catching on the mountain peaks. He stopped halfway down the hill and looked back. The castle windows glittered in the morning light.

He was sure he could find a cheap room down by the harbor, they always needed men on the boats. The course lay out of the bay, dead west over the calm ripples, toward the sunset. The net was cast when darkness had fallen—it sank soundlessly into the black sea and came up silvered. A long time ago, after he had gone out in the evening to fish for herring, he remembered Einar asking whether the sun ever got caught in the net.

At the last moment, he had decided to leave the letters behind. He had contemplated them for a long time before taking them out of his bag and wrapping them in a handkerchief. He left the shoebox on his desk, the note to the Chief on top of the shoebox, the letters next to it. Before he picked up his bags, he took one last look around his room. It already seemed foreign to him.

He didn't know how long the Chief had been standing in the doorway. They stared at one another for a while, then the old man cleared his throat.

"Is there anything I can do?"

He had never asked Kristjan about his life before they met and Kristjan was grateful to him for that. But now it was as if he understood everything without Kristjan having to explain.

"I left a note. A note and a shoebox. The note's for you."

"And the shoebox?"

There was silence while Kristjan tried to quell the lump in his throat.

"The shoebox and the letters are for my son."

The Chief was about to reach out his hand, then suddenly seemed to lose control of it, pulled it back.

264

"You don't think you can . . . ?"

Kristjan was on the point of groping for words to describe the thoughts he'd been trying for so long to understand; he was going to tell him that the explanation wasn't simple enough to be encapsulated in a single sentence, was aware of moving his lips, then stepped back inadvertently, retreated, and said merely:

"No, I can't. It's too late."

"Where to?" asked the old man after a long silence.

"I don't know. I'll leave the car . . ."

"Don't worry about the car."

Hearst looked down at his feet, then slowly straightened up and said, so quietly that he could hardly be heard:

"We all have to believe that we're decent. No matter what, we have to believe that. For there are no innocents; life is full of mysteries and mistakes. You're a good man, Christian. Take care of yourself. Take care of yourself, my friend."

The highway continued north along the coast, the ocean to the left, mountains to the right. But he had decided to stop here and see what happened. When he climbed up onto the rocks beside the turn-off he could see the part of the village that had been hidden before and felt even more certain that it would be a good place to stay.

He didn't jump, but eased his way carefully down from the rocks to the ground.

He shouldered his satchel and canvas bag, and set off in the direction of the village. The horse stopped grazing and looked up. As it sauntered away from the tree, still munching, the sun's rays spilled off its mane, over its back, and down its flanks. The leafy shadows vanished from its back, but Kristjan noticed that the shadow of the bird remained. He looked up at the sky but couldn't see it anywhere.

When the horse had disappeared into a hollow, the bird began to sing.

About the Author

Olaf Olafsson was born in Reykjavik, Iceland, in 1962, and studied physics as a Wien Scholar at Brandeis University. He is the author of two previous novels, *The Journey Home* and *Absolution,* which have been translated into fourteen languages. He lives in New York with his wife and two sons.